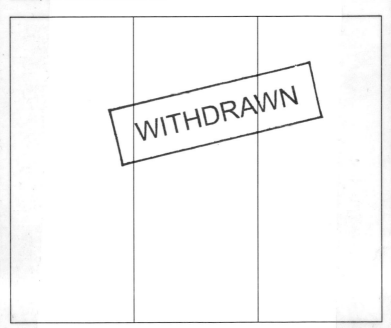

The
Lucky
Bottle

www.davidficklingbooks.com

Also by Chris Wormell

The Magic Place

The
Lucky
Bottle

Chris Wormell

David Fickling Books

31 Beaumont Street
Oxford OX1 2NP, UK

The Lucky Bottle
is a
DAVID FICKLING BOOK

First published in Great Britain in 2022 by
David Fickling Books,
31 Beaumont Street,
Oxford, OX1 2NP

Text and illustrations © Chris Wormell, 2022

978-1-78845-188-8

1 3 5 7 9 10 8 6 4 2

DAVID FICKLING BOOKS Reg. No. 8340307

A CIP catalogue record for this book is available from the British Library.

Typeset in Goudy by Falcon Oast Graphic Art Ltd

Printed and bound in Great Britain by Clays Ltd, Elcograf S.p.A

For Eliza, Daisy and Jack,
whose ship in a bottle was the germ of this story.

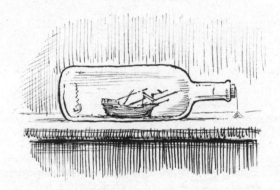

Chapter One
Storm

H ave you ever seen a model sailing ship inside a bottle? Yes? Well, did you know that such an object is called an 'impossible bottle'? Because, of course, *how* would one get a little ship, with masts and sails, in through the narrow neck of a bottle?

I don't know, do you?

This is the story of how the very first little ship got inside a bottle, and the person who put it there. It begins, however, not with a model but with a real, full-sized ship long ago on a faraway ocean, and on a wild night of tempest with waves so tall the ship looks almost as though it *were* a little model.

Decks awash, masts snapped, the ship tilts to this side and that, bow rising steeply high above the stern, as a vast

mountain ridge of ocean climbs into the sky, then tips and
folds, and crashes down upon the ship . . .

And it is gone.

A barrel bobs up to the surface . . .

A splintered fragment of mast; the broken bowsprit; the ship's wheel; shards of plank . . .

Then a hand . . .

Clutching, grasping, gripping the rope-ringed fragment of mast – *a head*, an arm: a young boy, spluttering, spitting, coughing, retching the salt sea, gasping in the wind and rain, clinging, clinging to the mast, white as a ghost amid the vast ink-black ocean . . .

Clinging, clinging, rising and falling with the waves.

Hours pass and the boy begins to slip in and out of consciousness. His body is numb with cold, frozen fingers loosening their grip, then . . .

'Jack!'

A voice calling his name, faint and distant amid the roar of the wind.

It comes again.

'Jack!'

Urgent, insistent. Wild hope flares in the boy's heart and he tries to call out but can only croak a cracked whisper. He seems to see his father splashing through the surf towards him, arms reaching out to rescue him as the foaming white breakers engulf him . . .

'Jack!'

And now he knows the voice is just a memory. The voice of his father from a long-ago sunny afternoon, on a distant beach.

There is no one to rescue him. He grips the rope-lashed mast, rising and falling with the hill-sized humpbacked swell.

Face down, cheek pressed into wet sand, Jack lay on a beach. A fly settled on the back of his neck. He opened an eye, and lifting his head, coughed, and spat out sand and sea. Then, sitting up, he raised a hand, shading his eyes against the glare, looking along the beach to right and left. Then out across the blue-green ocean. For a moment, he'd thought it might have been that other beach of long ago – that his father would be there, and his mother and sister. But no; he was alone with a few fragments of the broken ship scattered across the white sand.

Away to his right, Jack saw rocks rippling in the heat shimmer and, standing up, he walked towards them. On top of the rocks, he could now see a little of what lay behind the beach; an uneven stony land of sand and low-growing bushes and, farther off, a jumble of larger boulders rising up to form a small hill. All around was evidence of the storm: bushes, torn from the ground and tossed here and there, and others adorned with seaweed, shells and the broken bodies of small crabs. He could see no sign of any house or building. He tried to call out, but so dry and parched were his throat and mouth, his thin, cracked 'Hello!' was lost to the wind.

Below him, the beach veered sharply to the right and on to where more rocks shimmered in the heat. He climbed down, and as he walked, he called out – as best he could – the names of his shipmates: 'Captain Trelawney! . . . Mister Scobey! . . . Billy Braddock!' and so on and so on. But he heard no answer, and the thought gradually grew in Jack's mind that perhaps only he had survived the wreck, and that he was all alone on that strange shore. He blocked the thought; that was something he dared not think about. *There must be someone else, there must be!*

He began to run. But weak with exhaustion and hunger, he stumbled and fell, and lay sprawled on the sand, panting hard.

His outstretched right hand had come to rest on something smooth, hard and rounded. He lifted his head to look at the thing; a kind of bleached white dome, rising a little above the sand. A stone perhaps. Yet it did not *feel* like a stone. He sat up, curious, and began to dig around the thing . . . then jumped away in shock.

Staring up at him with eyeless sockets, was a human skull.

Chapter Two
A Castaway

Backing away, Jack turned and ran again, scrambling over rocks, heedless of cuts and scratches, the image of that gruesome object fixed before his eyes. Again, he tried to call out, desperate to discover that he was not alone. But still, no one answered his call.

Scrambling up the rocks at the top of the beach, he looked towards the low hillock of jumbled boulders. From there he would see a wider view of this country. He would see a house maybe, or a village? He set off towards the outcrop.

The bushes, he noticed, bore lime-green-coloured fruit, like strange knobbly pears. He picked one, raised it to his nose and sniffed it. Oddly, it had no smell whatever. Tentatively, he took a bite. Then pulled a face and spat.

'Yuck!'

It tasted horrible. He spat again, fearing he'd poisoned himself. It was the nastiest thing he had ever tasted in his life.

He threw the fruit away but was suddenly aware just how hungry he was. Achingly, *ravenously* hungry. And thirsty too, but he could see no sign of fresh water, nor anything else he might eat. If he could find a house or a farm, they would have food.

Stumbling and slipping on loose stones that scratched and cut the soles of his bare feet, he clambered over the uneven ground towards the outcrop of rocks. The bushes had sharp thorns and several times he ripped his shirt. Then he got a thorn stuck in his thumb and sat down on a large rock to squeeze the thumb and pull it out.

But the rock began to *move* . . .

It lifted him up and up, and with a yelp of sudden terror Jack leaped forward, tripping and falling – smashing his head on a stone. Stunned for a moment, he scrambled to turn over, but the rock – the *thing* – was upon him, trunk-like scaly legs planted either side of his body, lifting the 'rock' above him . . . and emerging from within, a blunt reptilian head on a wrinkled neck of sagging, leathery skin. The head stretched down towards Jack's face, swinging slowly from side to side. Black beady eyes examined him, a wide beak-like mouth snapped open, and the monster exhaled a long, rank hiss.

Then it lifted a great horny-toed foot, stepped over his body, and walked ponderously away.

For several minutes, Jack lay still, heart thumping high up in his throat, and only when all sounds of the monster's retreat had stilled did he get up. Some distance away, bushes moved, violently agitated, as the creature pushed its way among them.

Jack's limbs were still trembling, and his steps unsteady, as he began to climb one of the large boulders that formed the rocky outcrop. He wondered what other monsters lived in this barren and desolate land.

Scrambling up to the highest point of the hillock, he stood on the narrow summit and looked out over the land beyond.

What he saw filled Jack with dismay.

He spun around and looked back the way he'd come. Then turned full circle before falling to his knees with a pitiful wail of despair. In all directions, the view was the same. No house, no farm, no village. Nothing. He was surrounded by the vast, empty ocean.

He was on a tiny island.

Chapter Three
A Discovery

The awful truth of his predicament struck Jack like a blow to the chest. It seemed certain that he was doomed to spend the rest of his (probably very short) life on that tiny island, and his heart quailed. A great black void of loneliness came upon him, and a homesickness so acute, he wept uncontrollably.

Lying upon the rock, cheek against the stone, he thought of all that he had lost. Of his mother and his father and his sister, of his home back in England, of all the years of his past life . . . of all the things he would never see again.

But as the hours passed and the sun grew hotter and hotter, there came a time in the afternoon when the heat began to cook him, up there on his lofty perch, like toast on a grill. He stopped crying, rubbed a sleeve across his red swollen eyes, and looked about for a way to climb down. Somehow, he would escape from this wretched island – there must be a way, there *must*.

As he began to climb, he saw below him a pool of bright, clear water, glinting in the sun. A spring, and snaking away from it down towards the beach was a small stream. Slipping and sliding down the boulders, he ran to the pool, throwing himself on to the sand beside it and dipping his head to drink.

But before his lips touched the water, he stopped.

Inches from his face . . . was a giant human footprint.

Chapter Four
A Very Small Noise

He was not alone on this island.
But rather than relief, this discovery only brought
a shock of fear. Slowly he stood up and placed his own foot
beside the print in the sand. The footprint was more than
twice as large as his own. It could not belong to any of
Jack's shipmates. There were no *giants* among the crew of
the *Wessex*.

It was the footprint of a stranger. A stranger who was
hiding from Jack. For they must have known he was there.
Perhaps they were watching him at that very moment?

He quickly looked up at the boulders rising above the
pool, and then spun around, looking across the bushes
towards the beach. Nothing.

Turning back, he noticed that there were other prints,

less distinct, but clearly made by the same foot – or feet –
leading away from the pool and towards a mass of big rocks.
He followed them across the sand, and it was not until
he was standing right beside the great stones that Jack
discovered a gap where one rock overlapped another.
Between them, a narrow sandy path enclosed by sheer walls
wound its way towards the centre of the outcrop.

He had no idea who might be waiting for him at the end
of that path – or whether they were friend of foe – but he
realized, quite sensibly, that he had no chance of remaining hidden from the stranger, not for long at least – not on
this tiny island. And so, he began to walk down the narrow
sandy path, creeping along very slowly and trying to make
absolutely no noise at all, listening with all his might for the
tiniest sound. But heard nothing. The air was perfectly still

and even the crash of the distant waves was blocked out by the rocks around him. He almost felt he could hear the beating of his own heart, and though his inclination was to gulp in long, deep breaths to calm his nerves, he tried to breathe as slowly and as quietly as he could.

Not many yards along the path he was suddenly struck by the idea that the stranger might be waiting in ambush . . . to catch him. And then he remembered the skull on the beach and the word *cannibal* sprang into his mind . . .

He stopped.

Sheer terror engulfed him then. He could not go on. His heart seemed to stop and the breath froze in his lungs. He began to shake.

And at that very moment, he heard a noise.

Only a very small noise, but a noise so odd – so utterly out of place on that desolate island – he was confounded and waited for the noise to come again.

And there it was!

In an instant, Jack's fears seemed to evaporate . . . and he smiled.

He was absolutely certain that he could hear the sound of someone reading a book . . .

Chapter Five
The Reader

It was the sound of a *page* being turned. A slight sound, but quite distinct. And a sound that Jack somehow found hugely reassuring. He crept forward again with much more confidence.

Just up ahead, he could now see sunlight shining down on the sand and he guessed that the path must widen there. Mustering his courage, he walked forward and stepped out into the light.

A square space surrounded by high vertical rocks opened out around him. And sitting on a wooden chair in the middle of it, was a man doing exactly as Jack had guessed. He was reading a book.

A *huge* man with an immense black beard. He made no sign that he was aware of Jack's presence and continued to read his book. Jack stood stock still. Then, when he'd made his mind up to say something and was about to clear his throat, the man raised a forefinger and without lifting his head, said:

'Please excuse me for just a moment. I have only this page to finish – it's the very *last* page of the book!'

Jack was flummoxed. He opened his mouth to speak, but up went the stranger's finger, so he closed it again.

He wasn't frightened. Not much. Chiefly, he was filled with an overwhelming sense of relief; the man sounded friendly. He had a voice like deep, slow music, a warm and comfortable voice. And so strong was Jack's sense of reassurance and hope, that he was suddenly overcome with emotion and his face crumpled a little, and his eyes filled with tears.

'Finished!' declared the stranger, closing his book with a snap and laying it on the sand. 'A wonderful story – and very instructive! I recommend it!' Then, looking across at Jack and seeing his tears, he leaped to his feet and cried, 'Oh my! Oh my! Dear, dear me!'

And now Jack *was* alarmed; the man towered above him almost blocking out the sun. He backed away down the path a little.

'Forgive me,' said the man in a voice filled with remorse. 'I did not mean to frighten you.' And then he bowed so low his great beard brushed against the sand, and straightening up, he said, 'I mean you no harm. Please excuse my rude and callous behaviour.' Then he reached out an enormous hand towards Jack, and said, 'I am honoured to meet you, Mister . . . ?'

Jack sniffed, wiped his sleeve across his face, and stuttered, 'Er . . . Jack – Jack Bobbin,' then raised his own hand.

'A pleasure, Jack Bobbin!' said the stranger, gently shaking Jack's hand. 'My name is . . . My name is . . . Goodness me, what *is* my name?'

He seemed altogether at a loss.

After a long pause, the man said, 'Oh dear, it's been so many years since I had need of a name, I seem to have forgotten mine – the one I was last using, at least. I'll have to *choose* a name.'

As the stranger spoke, Jack began to wobble a little; exhaustion and hunger as well as immense relief were beginning to overcome him.

'Good heavens! What am I thinking – sit down, young man, sit down!' cried the man, guiding Jack towards the chair. 'And here, have some water.' He picked up a bottle from the sand, uncorked it and handed it to Jack.

'One moment,' the man said, and disappeared into what must have been a cave in one corner of the sandy square. Beside it was a large pile of empty bottles, similar the one Jack was now holding.

When the man reappeared, he was carrying a second

chair which he planted in the sand beside Jack, and said: 'Please forgive my rudeness, Jack – I've lived alone too long and forgotten all my manners! But tell me your story – what happened to you? Were you caught in the storm? Was your ship wrecked?'

Jack nodded.

'And you are alone?'

Jack nodded again.

The man was silent for a while, then asked, 'Did you have family or friends on the ship?'

Jack shook his head.

'You were with the crew, perhaps?'

Again, Jack nodded. 'But I didn't really have friends among them. Not good friends.'

'A cabin boy?'

Once more, Jack nodded.

'Forgive me, but you seem very young.'

'I lied. I'm ten and a half, but I told Captain Trelawney I was twelve, just small for my age.'

The man nodded now. He seemed to sense that the memory of the storm and shipwreck were still painfully fresh in Jack's mind and changed the subject.

'Forgive me for not coming to your aid sooner.'

Jack looked up at the man, puzzled.

'I was out at the pool filling that bottle when I heard your wail – from up on the rocks above. It gave me the shock of my life! I thought for a moment it was some strange bird, then I heard you begin to cry. I would have come up to you but was wary of introducing myself *there*. The summit of the rock is a rather precarious spot; I feared the sight of my approach might result in a dreadful accident! Better that you should come and find me, I thought. Forgive me.'

Jack smiled. The sight of the giant stranger climbing up towards him would certainly have given him a fright.

'You saw my footprints by the pool, I suppose?'

Jack nodded. And then an idea seemed to occur to the man and with a laugh, he bent down and picked up the book he'd been reading.

Inscribed on of the book's spine, in fine gold lettering, were the words: *The Life and Strange Surprizing Adventures of Robinson Crusoe, of York, Mariner* by Daniel Defoe.

'Would you believe, Jack, this book is the story of a castaway on a desert island? It's given me an idea for the name I will choose. The castaway is a chap called Robinson Crusoe, and in the story he saves another fellow from being eaten by cannibals and befriends him. He calls the fellow Friday – Man Friday, as Friday is the day on which they met. And as it happens, they meet in a similar fashion to the way we two have met; he finds a footprint in the sand! Today isn't a Friday, however, it's a Thursday – I keep a very careful calendar, Jack.'

'Do you want me to call you *Thursday*?' asked Jack.

'Why no,' replied the man, 'I was thinking *Robinson*: the chap who does the rescuing.'

Chapter Six
Supper

'You must be famished, Jack,' said the man – *Robinson* – standing up and laying the book on his chair. 'What about some supper?'

Before Jack could answer, Robinson disappeared into the cave once more. A moment later he reappeared with a canvas bag slung over his shoulder and what seemed to be a broom handle with a large fork attached to one end.

'My fishing spear!' he declared, with a broad smile. 'We shall light a fire and cook supper down on the beach. Follow me!'

He set off down the narrow, sandy pathway. Jack followed.

'I'll try my luck in the sea, Jack,' said Robinson, as they stepped on to the beach at the point where the stream ran down across the sand. 'You collect some wood for a fire

– there are plenty of dry branches lying about under the bushes.'

Robinson walked down to the sea with his spear and climbed on to a low pier of rock, jutting out into the waves.

By the time Jack had enough wood for a decent-sized fire, Robinson was walking back up the beach carrying two plump fish. Laying them on the sand, he handed Jack a tinderbox he'd taken from his canvas bag.

'You get the fire going, Jack, while I gut and clean the fish.'

Jack knew how to use a tinderbox, and with dry leaves as tinder and twigs as kindling, he soon had the fire crackling away nicely. Robinson gutted and cleaned the fish then skewered them and placed them over the fire. Almost instantly a wonderful aroma filled the air.

The sun had sunk below the horizon by the time they'd finished eating, and darkness had crept up all around them. Jack was sucking the fish bones for any last morsels of flesh, when a disturbing thought struck him.

'Er . . . Mister Robinson, sir – there aren't any *cannibals* on the island, are there?'

'Cannibals? Goodness me no! What a horrible idea!' said Robinson, aghast.

'It's just that I saw the skull . . .'

'Skull?'

'I think it's back there, beyond the stream.' Jack pointed away into the darkness behind him.

Without a word, Robinson stood up and walked off in the direction Jack indicated. Jack jumped up and followed him.

The moon was now high in the sky, and away from the fire, the beach and the waves were rimmed with a silvery glow.

'There!' cried Jack, pointing ahead to where the white dome rose above the sand.

Robinson bent down over the gruesome relic and gave a low whistle. 'I've never come across this fellow before!' he said. 'The storm must have shifted the sand and uncovered it.'

The skull looked particularly creepy in the moonlight. Jack was glad he was not alone.

'We shall have to rebury the poor fellow a little deeper,' said Robinson. 'Though not now of course – we'll come down in the morning. I wonder who they were?'

They left the skull shining grimly in the moonlight and walked back to the fire, which was now just glowing embers, and while Jack washed the plates and forks in the stream, Robinson scraped out a hole in the sand with his enormous hands, and pushed in the embers along with the fish bones. Once he'd covered it over and smoothed down the sand, no trace remained of their supper.

Picking up the canvas bag and spear, he said, 'Time for bed, I think. You are most welcome to share my cave, Jack.'

Jack, of course, accepted this offer and they climbed the rocks at the top of the beach and set off for the rocky outcrop, now just a vague outline on the horizon. In the dark, Jack found it impossible to follow Robinson's footprints as he had done earlier and almost immediately, he stumbled on a loose rock and fell.

'Would you like some help?' asked Robinson, pulling Jack to his feet once more.

Jack nodded, vaguely wondering what 'help' meant. Before he could ask, Robinson had handed him the spear, caught him under the armpits, and swung Jack up on to his massive shoulders as easily as a sack of feathers.

Utterly exhausted, Jack began to nod off long before they reached the cave. He had a memory of squeezing down the narrow path, then he must have dropped off altogether, for he dreamed that he was laid down on a great four-poster bed with a thick mattress and the softest pillows . . .

Chapter Seven
The Cave

It wasn't a dream. The next morning Jack woke to find that he *was* lying in a great four-poster bed on a thick mattress, his head resting on the softest pillows! He sat up, and for a moment wondered where on earth he was. This surely wasn't the cave he'd seen the day before. All around him were things such as one might expect to find in a grand house – a *very* grand house; fine chairs with legs carved like spiralling serpents, an ornate table standing on a richly patterned oriental rug, a leather Chesterfield sofa, a bow-fronted chest of drawers with shiny brass handles, wardrobes and cupboards and armchairs, stacks of blue-patterned plates piled up on sideboards, china teapots, candlesticks, crockery and cutlery; pots and pans and pewter mugs, and in one corner, a tall grandfather clock gently tick-tocking away – and possibly telling the right time.

And yet, he *was* in the cave. For looking up, he could see the rough rock ceiling above his head. And the floor, where it was visible between the rugs, was sand.

He stood up and began to walk around, picking up objects and marvelling at all he saw. The cave was large, very large. It seemed to slope down and must have stretched underground far beyond the extent of the rocky outcrop. How far, he couldn't guess, but all he could see of it was filled with fine furniture and wonderful objects.

Until that moment Jack had assumed that Robinson was a castaway – a sailor, washed ashore just as he had been. But this was surely not the case. Robinson must have *wished* to come to this island. He must have brought all these things with him. And to own such things, he must surely be a very rich man.

But why would such a man choose to live in a cave on a tiny island?

Jack's eye suddenly fell upon something that looked altogether out of place among all the grand and marvellous things in that cave. Lying on a small table was a rough-looking stone. He wondered why it was there. Then he noticed marks on the cave wall above the table – scratched lines covering quite a large area, as if someone had spent some time inscribing a pattern there. He guessed that the stone had been used to make the marks and walked over to have a closer look.

The lines were not a random pattern. They were arranged in neat rows of seven, one row on top of another so that they formed tall columns. He began to count the rows and suddenly he understood what he was looking at.

Seven scratched lines in columns of fifty-two rows – the lines were days, the rows were weeks, and the columns were years.

He was looking at Robinson's calendar!

Standing back, he counted the columns. Robinson had been living on this island for nineteen and a half years.

Chapter Eight
Yuckies

Outside, Jack found Robinson sitting on a rock by the pool, reading.

'Thank you, sir,' he said, sitting down beside him.

Robinson looked up with a smile. 'For what?' he asked.

'Thank you for the loan of your bed, sir – and for supper. I'm sorry, I forgot my manners last night.' He suddenly felt the need to be more respectful; this man might well be a person of some importance.

Robinson laughed. 'You're welcome to the bed; it's much too small for me – I sleep on a straw mattress on the other side of the cave. And there's no need to worry about manners *here*. And no need to call me *sir* either, or *Mister*. Just Robinson will do fine.'

Jack nodded, though he was puzzled as to why Robinson

would have a bed that was too small for him to sleep in. He was about to ask whether there was somebody else on the island, when Robinson picked up two of the knobbly, pear-like fruits that Jack had found so disgusting the day before.

'Breakfast!' he declared.

Jack pulled a face. 'You don't eat *yuckies* do you? They're horrible!'

'Yuckies?' queried Robinson. 'Is that what you call them? An excellent name – perfectly descriptive; they are, indeed, yucky! I've never called them anything myself, but henceforth – yuckies they shall be!' He took a bite from one of the fruits and chewed unenthusiastically, then, after swallowing his mouthful, said, 'One must eat fruit, as I'm sure you know, Jack, and as these are the only fruit to be found on this island, I eat them. I can't say I *enjoy* them – I don't; they're the foulest, most unpleasant things I've ever eaten in my life – and one *never* gets used to them, *ever*. But, eat them I do. And you must too.' He handed the other fruit to Jack.

Jack looked at it with distaste. 'What if you cook them?' Jack asked. 'Do they taste better then?'

'Not a bit,' said Robinson bluntly. 'I've baked them, fried them and boiled them, but they're just as bad. I've chopped them up and mixed them with other things, but they overpower and spoil any dish they are added to. There's nothing good to be said for them, except that they are not poisonous. Now eat up! We have some grave digging to do.'

Chapter Nine
The Skeleton

A short time later they stood on the beach, looking down at the skull.

'No good just piling up sand on top of the fellow,' said Robinson. 'It'd soon blow away again. I think we shall have to disinter them to do the thing properly.'

Jack wondered what 'disinter' meant.

'Dig them up,' said Robinson, as if reading Jack's thoughts. 'That's if there *are* any more of them – bones, I mean. It might just be a skull.'

They knelt down, one either side of where they assumed the rest of the bones would lie – if there were any – and began to dig with their hands. After making a few rather tentative scrapes, Jack jumped back with a start. He'd uncovered a rib. There *were* more bones. He'd never seen a skeleton before, not a human one, and sat back and watched, a little horrified, as Robinson scooped away the sand methodically until, after ten minutes or so, the whole skeleton lay revealed.

All the bones seemed to be intact, and here and there a few faded scraps of cloth were wrapped about them. Scattered among the bones were a number of brass buttons and the buckle of a belt, and lying beside one of the long leg bones, a cutlass, almost rusted away to nothing.

'I'm guessing by the cutlass it's a "he",' said Robinson, picking up a long-handled spade he'd brought along. 'Might not be, though – we'll never know for sure. But the cutlass suggests a seaman of some sort.'

He stood up and began to dig a hole beside the skeleton.

'I always had the feeling that someone else had lived on this island before me,' he said as he worked. 'One or two things I've come upon over the years have suggested the existence of a former resident – perhaps this is he?'

Jack could see that the body had not been properly buried; the limbs were more spread out than they would have been if they had been put into a grave. He'd either been washed ashore or had fallen or lain down on the beach and died, and over the years the sand had covered him.

'That ought to do,' said Robinson after he'd been digging for about fifteen minutes. The hole was now four feet deep and easily long enough for the skeleton.

'Shall *I* move him?' he asked, giving Jack a questioning glance. Jack nodded; he had no wish to touch the bones.

Robinson began to move the skeleton, reassembling it, bone by bone, at the bottom of the hole. He'd moved the skull and several of the vertebrae when Jack said:

'Wait a minute – what's that? I think he's holding something in his hand!'

The bones of the skeleton's right hand were indeed clenched into a kind of fist around something. Robinson, who was standing in the hole, bent forward to look closer.

'I believe you're right,' he said, and carefully began to lift up the various phalanges and metacarpal bones to reveal what it was the man had been holding: a small scrap of waxy paper. He picked it up and unfolded it – though it was more screwed-up than folded – then held it where both he and Jack could see it. There were words and numbers written on the scrap of paper.

'What do you think it means?' asked Jack.

'I don't know,' admitted Robinson. 'It's been written with

a pencil, and not very neatly – he was probably in a hurry. The figures at the top are clearly a record of latitude and longitude – at least that's how I read them. I can't make any sense of  the words, though. "On the she"?' He shook his head and frowned. 'This is only a fragment, mind; just the corner of a larger piece of paper – do you see? I imagine all would be clear if we had the rest of the sheet.' He scanned the ground around the skeleton, looking for any more scraps of paper, but neither he nor Jack could see any.

'Is there anything on the other side?' asked Jack.

Robinson turned over the paper. The other side, however, was blank. 'We'll keep it anyway,' he said, carefully folding the paper and putting it into his pocket. 'You never know . . .'

He then set about transferring the rest of the bones to the newly dug hole and had almost finished when Jack spotted the glint of something in the sand where the bones of the ribcage had been lying. With a sudden thrill of excitement, he reached down and dug it out. It was a gold doubloon, shining like a fragment of sun.

'Ha! Buried treasure!' cried Robinson. 'That's a lucky find!'

Jack had never seen a gold coin before – at least, none

as large and heavy as this one. It did indeed look and feel like treasure. He rubbed it with his shirt sleeve and gazed in wonder as it sparkled even brighter. On one side was the profile of what he assumed to be a king, while on the other was a kind of cross. The words around the edge of the coin were almost worn away, and the date too.

'Can I keep it, do you think?' he asked Robinson, expectantly.

'Most certainly, Jack! I'm sure this fellow wouldn't mind – *he* has no need of it any more!'

Jack beamed, and while he sat, gazing at the golden coin, Robinson began shovelling sand back into the hole, reburying the skeleton along with the buttons and rusted cutlass. When he'd finished, he walked to the top of the beach to find a rock that might serve as a gravestone.

'What shall we call him?' he said, returning a few minutes later with a large, flat stone. *An Unknown Sailor* seems rather anonymous.'

Jack shrugged. 'Mister Bones?' he suggested, half in jest. 'That's all that's left, just bones.'

'True. What about *Billy Bones*? That has a certain ring to it.'

Jack nodded, and Robinson scratched the words, 'HERE LIES BILLY BONES' on the rock with a small sharp stone, before laying it on top of the grave.

'May you now rest in peace, Mister Bones,' he said.

Chapter Ten
Caliban

After reburying the skeleton, they walked around the beach to see what could be salvaged from the wreckage of Jack's ship – the *Wessex*.

'Robinson,' said Jack as they walked. 'I saw your calendar – on the wall of the cave. You've been here for nineteen and a half years, haven't you?'

'I have,' replied Robinson.

'And have you been alone for all that time?' Jack was unable to hide the note of incredulity in his voice. He felt sure he would have gone mad being alone for so long.

'Indeed,' replied Robinson. 'Except for Caliban.'

'*Caliban?* Is there someone *else* on the island? Was it Caliban's bed I slept in?'

Robinson laughed. 'Goodness me, no! Tortoises have no

need of beds.'

'A tortoise?'

'Great big chap, bit like a giant lizard with a shell on his back.'

'Yes, I met him!' exclaimed Jack. 'At least, I think I did – unless there are others? I sat on him; I thought he was a rock!'

'Dear me, I'm sure he didn't appreciate that.'

'No, I don't think he did. He's huge! He's as big as an upturned bathtub! *Are* there others?'

'No, only Caliban. I suppose there must have been others once; a whole colony perhaps, but Caliban is the only one left. I've tried to strike up a friendship with the beast many times but to no avail. In all the nineteen and a half years I've been here he's remained aloof and haughty. He seems to have a distinct loathing for humanity. Unless, of course, it's just me.'

'I don't think he liked me much either,' said Jack, remembering the look in the monster's eye and its angry hiss.

When they reached the place where Jack had come ashore, they dragged the fragments of mast, the frayed ropes and splintered planks up the beach, away from any danger of being taken by the tide. There wasn't much worth salvaging though. Certainly not enough wood to make a raft, which had been Jack's hope.

Looking at the wreckage, the horror of the storm was suddenly fresh in Jack's mind again and he began to

tremble. He sat down on the sand and Robinson sat down beside him, putting an arm around his shoulders. Neither spoke, but with Robinson's reassuring and gentle presence, Jack's fears were stilled. In an effort to shift his mind from the storm, he asked, 'How did you get all your things into the cave, Robinson? Your furniture and stuff. The bed and the wardrobe and all the big things – they couldn't possibly fit down the narrow path. Is there another way in?'

'There is,' said Robinson. 'From above! One by one I carried each item of furniture up to the top of one of the Skittles and lowered them down on to the sand below . . .'

'Skittles?'

'Yes, that's the name I've given the larger rocks above the cave; there are nine of them standing in a bunch around my secret courtyard.'

Jack nodded, then asked, 'But . . . but *how* did you carry them?'

'Well, the bed was in pieces,' replied Robinson, 'so that wasn't difficult. But the other things I carried on my back.'

Jack had a mental image of Robinson scaling the rocky outcrop with a wardrobe tied to his back. He couldn't believe that anyone but this man could do such a thing.

Then it suddenly occurred to him that a large wardrobe might easily make the beginnings of a raft . . . He didn't say anything, however, not yet.

'But what about *getting* all your things to this island?' he asked, and then, eagerly, as another idea occurred to him,

'Have you got a *ship*? Have you got a boat in a secret bay somewhere?' A boat would be much better than a raft.

'I'm afraid not,' replied Robinson, shaking his head. 'You see, *I* didn't bring them here at all. They were all washed up on the beach.'

'Washed up?'

Robinson nodded. 'Yes, washed up. And luckily, they were all in more-or-less watertight packing crates, so were mostly undamaged.'

'So . . . they're not really *your* things at all.'

'Well, they are *now*, I suppose. Finders keepers and all that. But originally, they all belonged to a man named John Millington, and I know that because I found his name inscribed on the book plates on the inside cover of all the books I have. I imagine he had sold up all his lands in America and was returning to England. All his belongings were in the cargo hold of a ship called the *New Horizon*.'

'How do you know that?'

'Because, Jack, I was also on that same ship.'

Jack thought he understood now. 'So, the ship was wrecked in a storm, and you were washed ashore on this island like me!'

Robinson shook his head. 'No, Jack. As far as I know the *New Horizon* is still afloat. I was not, strictly speaking, a passenger on that ship. I was in the cargo hold with all the packing crates, and along with all those packing crates, I was thrown overboard by *pirates* . . .'

Chapter Eleven
Bad Bob

'Pirates!' exclaimed Jack.

'Indeed,' replied Robinson.

'But . . . how? What happened?'

Jack loved stories about pirates.

'Aha!' replied Robinson with a laugh and a wink. 'You'll have to wait a little to discover that, Jack. It's a jolly good story, and much better told by firelight after supper this evening!'

Jack shrugged; that was what his father and mother always said: 'Stories are for bedtime.'

In the meantime, Robinson took Jack on a tour of the island and told him about the various animals and birds that lived there and pointed out particular landmarks. He showed Jack where seaweed and shellfish could be gathered, and where he collected eggs from a colony of gulls at the northern tip.

He spoke with enthusiasm about the island and with evident pride. Jack, however, still thought it a desolate and lonesome place. There were no trees, and really nothing at all to relieve the monotony of rocks and bushes and sand. Its only notable features were the outcrop of rocks where the cave was, the pool of fresh water, and the stream.

As they made their way back to the cave late in the afternoon, Jack asked, 'If you didn't come here on purpose, Robinson, have you never tried to build a raft and escape and go home?'

'Escape?' replied Robinson, a little surprised. 'But this *is* my home. I'm perfectly happy here!'

Jack was somehow dismayed by this reply. He suddenly felt a little quake inside himself, an echo of the desperate homesickness of the day before.

'But . . . but *I* want to escape, Robinson,' he said. 'I don't think I could be happy here. *I* want to get back home.'

'Of course, you do, Jack!' cried Robinson. 'And so you shall! I may not have a boat or a raft, but we'll think of something else – be sure of it!'

Jack, however, was not so sure. Without a boat or a raft, was there any other way to escape?

That evening, Robinson carried a large pan down to the beach, and resting it on stones above a fire, cooked the sea-weed and shellfish they'd gathered earlier with a dash of rum, cracking several gull's eggs on top to finish it off. It was delicious. And when they'd finished, and not a morsel remained in the pan, Jack said: 'Tell me about the pirates, Robinson. I love pirate stories. Old Ma Rollock used to tell them. They were my favourite.'

'Who is Old Ma Rollock?' asked Robinson.

'She's someone who used to tell us wonderful stories. Sailors' stories, about voyages to amazing places on the far side of the world; of whales and sea monsters and pirates. And they were all true, she said. She was old when I knew her and lived in a cottage by the shore in a little fishing village, but when she was younger, she'd kept an inn on the quay at Falmouth, where sailors from all over the world would drink. She'd listened to their stories for most of her life. I used to listen to Old Ma Rollock, sitting with the children of the fisherman on the rocks outside her cottage. She knew lots of stories about *Robert the Bad*.'

'Who's he?' asked Robinson.

'You know – the pirate, Robinson! You must have heard of him. He was the wickedest pirate ever! Robert the Bad – but mostly people just called him Bad Bob.'

Robinson shook his head. 'No, I don't think I've ever come across that name. I've heard of another pirate with the initials BB, you don't mean him, do you? What was he called . . . Black Beard, that's it!'

'No, no, not him. He had a beard, of course. Bad Bob didn't. He *hated* beards. Old Ma Rollock used to begin her

stories: *No eye, no leg, no hand, and no beard! Chin as smooth as a baby's bottom!*'

'No leg, did you say? And no hand?'

'Yes. No leg, no hand, and no eye. Bad Bob had a wooden leg, a hook and an eyepatch . . .'

'Really? That's very curious, he sounds a lot like the pirate captain in *my* story. I know for certain *he* had a wooden leg, and I'm almost sure he had a hook instead of a hand too. Perhaps he was your *Bad Bob*. Did he have a parrot?'

'Yes. It was called Lord Boothby. It was an ugly black bird with a completely bald head like a vulture, and it spoke! It said, *"I'll peck out your eyes! I'll peck out your eyes!"* And other horrible things like that.'

'Ha ha! It *was* him!' cried Robinson. 'It *must* have been. There can't be two pirates with such a bird! I heard those very words not six inches from my right ear!'

Jack shook his head. 'But, Robinson, your pirate couldn't possibly have been Bad Bob.'

'Why not?'

'Because of your *beard*! Your enormous black beard! Or didn't you have one then?'

'I did have one.'

'Then it wasn't Bad Bob. If Bad Bob had seen your beard, you wouldn't be alive today! I told you – he really *hated* beards. He couldn't bear them. Old Ma Rollock used to say: *The sight of a beard would drive Bad Bob into a tremendous rage, and it would be instantly removed – usually with the head of its owner still attached! Woe betide any of Bad Bob's crew who forgot to pack a razor . . .*'

'Curious. Why did he hate beards so?'

'I don't know,' replied Jack. 'I'm not sure Old Ma Rollock did either. Perhaps because he couldn't grow one himself?'

'Very odd,' said Robinson with a frown. 'Nevertheless, I still say my pirate *was* Bad Bob. But let me begin at the beginning . . .'

Chapter Twelve
Robinson's Story

'I was a stowaway hiding in the cargo hold of the *New Horizon*, and had been there for almost a week, very hungry and very thirsty, when I was woken one morning by the sound of a pistol shot. It was followed by more shots – along with the clash of cutlasses and the cries and shouts of battle. Cowering in my dark corner, I thought at first the crew had mutinied and wondered what I should do. And then, as suddenly as it had begun, the noise ceased, and all was deathly quiet. Until, from up on the deck above me, there came a strange, squawky voice . . . *"I'll peck out your eyes! I'll peck out your eyes!"*

'It was accompanied by the distinctive footstep of some-one with a wooden leg walking across the deck, thumping it down with a – *Whack! – Whack! – Whack!*

'In all the time I'd been hiding in the hold, I had never heard anyone with a wooden leg walking on the deck. I guessed that the ship had been taken by pirates!

'There were more footsteps – all over the ship; the pirates must have been searching for any remaining crew or passengers. They would surely search the cargo hold . . .

'I needed a better hiding place! And then I remembered that one of the packing crates had been opened and not nailed shut. Earlier that week, in the middle of the night, someone had crept down into the hold and prised it open. They had carried a small candle, so that I was able to see them take something from the crate, and though I couldn't see what it was, I'd distinctly heard the pop of a cork being extracted. When they'd gone, I investigated the crate for myself and found that it was full of bottles, bedded down among quantities of straw. I uncorked one. They were bottles of rum.

'Anyway, as the pirates hurried about on the deck above, I found the crate again and, thankfully, the lid was still loose. As quickly as I could, I emptied the crate, stuffing the bottles and straw in a dark corner, before climbing in and lifting on the lid above me. It was a tight squeeze. In fact, I *didn't* really fit, and found the lid would not lie flat unless firmly pulled down. I'd only just managed to do this when the pirates entered the hold –'

'How?' interrupted Jack.

'How what?'

'How did you hold down the lid firmly when you were *inside* the crate? You couldn't nail it down.'

'Ah, quite right. I did it with *this*, Jack!'

Robinson raised his right hand and pointed to the darkening sky above. Jack looked up.

'What's up there?'

'Not up there – *this*! My finger. I used my finger to secure the lid. There was a small knot hole in it, and I was able

to poke my finger through the hole and grip the lid on the outside, and thus hold it firmly in place.'

'But the pirates could have *seen* your finger.'

'Indeed! I had to take that chance; they would certainly have noticed if the crate was *open*.'

Jack nodded. 'What happened then?'

'Well, I knew there were two pirates, for though I couldn't see them, I could hear their voices. "Not much down here," said one, and then, "Just boxes," said the other. A moment later . . . *Whack! – Whack! – Whack!* The pirate with the wooden leg was coming down the stairs into the hold.

"Nothin' 'ere, Cap'n," said the first pirate.

"Only boxes," added the second.

"Boxes!" roared Wooden Leg (he "roared" a lot).

"*Boxes! Boxes! Boxes!*" echoed the parrot, which – as you say – must have been on his shoulder.

"What's in 'em?" demanded Wooden Leg.

"Dunno, Cap'n," said the first pirate.

"Well, you'd better 'ave a look in 'em!" replied Wooden Leg.

"'*Ave a look, 'ave a look, 'ave a look!*" squawked the parrot.

'Someone ran out of the hold – looking for something to open the crates with, I guessed. They must have returned with an axe, for moments later I heard the splintering of wood.

"Plates, Cap'n," said the first voice. "That's what's in 'em. Plates and cups, Cap'n."

"Plates!"

"An' cups, Cap'n – with a rather nice design of . . ."

'SMASH! – the sound of breaking crockery.

"I DON'T WANT *PLATES!*"

'More breaking crockery.

"What's in *that* one?"

'More splintering wood.

"Chair, Cap'n. A jolly nice leather . . ."

'Ripping and slashing sounds – as if the chair was being attacked with a cutlass.

"I DON'T WANT A *CHAIR!*"

'More crates were broken into with the axe, and all the while the parrot was squawking: "*Smash 'em, smash 'em, smash 'em!*" and "*Crack 'em, crack 'em, crack 'em!*" And then the *Whack! – Whack! – Whack!* of Wooden Leg's steps came to a halt right beside *my* crate.

"Open up this one!" he ordered, and I braced myself, expecting to feel the blade of the axe, smashing into the crate . . .

'But then Wooden Leg said: "Hold on! What's in that pile of straw over there? Fetch a lantern. FETCH A LANTERN, I SAY!"

'A lantern must have been fetched, for a few moments later Wooden Leg declared, "It's *RUM!*"

'He must have picked up one of the bottles I'd taken out of the crate.

"Bottles of rum! *Lots of 'em!*" he roared. "And there'll be more in some of these crates – be sure of it! Chuck out all the other junk, lads, just hold on to the crates of *rum*!"

'His steps receded as he made his way to the companionway. Then suddenly he bellowed: "PUT DOWN THAT AXE!"

'And I heard the sound of an axe falling to the floor. Then silence.

"You break one bottle and lose one drop of rum, and I'll feed yer eyeballs to me bird!" He spoke very quietly, his voice cutting the air like a razor. It sent a shiver down my spine.

"S-sorry, Cap'n," said the second pirate, who must have been the one wielding the axe. "I weren't thinkin'. But . . . but how we gonna see what's in 'em if we don't smash 'em open?"

"Don't need to smash 'em open, stupid!" replied Wooden Leg, icily. "Not now you've got a *lantern*. Read the labels, numbskull!"

'There was a moment's silence, then the second pirate said, "Er . . . I can't read, Cap'n."

'Wooden Leg growled ominously. "What about you?" This was presumably directed at the first pirate.

"Er . . . a little, Cap'n," said he.

"Read that!" Wooden Leg must have been pointing at one of the crates.

"Bo . . . bo . . . bo . . ." stuttered the first pirate.

"*Books*, numbskull! It says books! Bee – oh – oh – kay

– ess! BOOKS! Now you say it!"

"Bee – oh . . ."

"That's right, *books*! Now we don't want any of that rubbish, so that goes over the side. What you're lookin' for is *this* . . ."

'I then heard the clink of metal against glass. It must have been the captain tapping the bottle he was holding with his hook – at least, I'm assuming he had a hook.

"See what it says there?" he said. "It says RUM. That's the word you're looking for. Are – you – em. Got it?"

'The first pirate clearly hadn't got it. "Am I *who*, Cap'n?" he replied.

"ARE – YOU – EM!" roared Wooden Leg. "RUM, you jellyfish-brained idiot! *Are – you – em!*"

"Oh! Sorry, Cap'n. Are – you – em. Rum! Got it!"

"That's what you're looking for. Everything else goes overboard! And while you're sortin' all this out, I'm off to me cabin to sample a drop of the stuff!"

'I heard him walking away towards the stairs.

'Then suddenly the parrot squawked: *"I can see a finger! I can see a finger!"*

Chapter Thirteen
A Sore Finger

'M y heart almost stopped. My first impulse, of course, was to withdraw my finger from the hole. But I knew if I did that the lid would spring up a little. They were bound to see it move. I held my breath and waited.

'And *nothing* happened.

'At least, there was no sign that those pirates had taken any notice of the parrot. It was as if it hadn't spoken a word. Wooden Leg began to climb the steps out of the hold.

"*There's a finger on that crate!*" squawked the parrot, excitedly. "*There's a finger on that crate!*"

'But still, the pirates ignored it. *I* could hear quite clearly what the bird was saying, but they seemed utterly oblivious to it.

'Suddenly there was a clatter of flapping wings, then the

parrot was on top of the crate pecking at my finger! Despite the pain, I dared not move it. Wooden Leg cursed, and the *Whack! – Whack! – Whack!* of his footsteps approached the crate . . .

'I braced myself, intending to burst out of the crate like an enormous Jack-in-the-box, but Wooden Leg roared: "Come 'ere, Boothby! And cease thy confounded chatter!"

'And then the parrot was no longer pecking at my finger. And nor was it squawking – Wooden Leg must have grabbed it by the throat.

'Unbelievably, neither he, nor the other two pirates had seen my finger! And while Wooden Leg stomped off with his parrot and his bottle of rum, more pirates came down into the hold. I could hear crates being shifted, and guessed they were being put into a net and hoisted up out of the hold, swung over the side of the ship and dropped into the sea. There was a chance I might escape if my crate was dropped into the sea, but surely, they wouldn't do that – my crate had been full of *rum*!

'I braced myself again, ready to burst out upon the pirates and take my chances. But as they approached my crate, I heard the first pirate say, "Bee – oh . . . that's *books*, that is. We don't want none o' that!"

'And incredibly, my crate was lifted into the net and hauled up out of the hold. I was just beginning to believe that luck was on my side and that I was about to escape from that ship, when a voice said, "Hold on! Hold on! What's that? I can see a bloody *finger* on top of that crate!" Again, I prepared to leap out, but then: "So? What of it?" said yet another voice. "There's a whole hand lying over there – I chopped that one off meself! Release the net!"

'And – *SPLASH* – my crate fell into the ocean!

'I'm rather heavy, Jack, and the crate sank down so low, it was soon full of water and I was obliged to let go of the lid and clamber out. Luckily, I was, by then, some distance from the ship and was not spotted.

'I clung to that crate for two long days, and I'd almost given up hope of rescue when – wonder of wonders – my feet touched solid ground!

'I'd come ashore on this island!'

Jack was silent for some moments after Robinson had finished his story. It was such an incredible tale he wondered if it was really true, but looking down at Robinson's right index finger, he saw the that it still bore the scars of the parrot's pecking. It must be true.

'But why did they throw *your* crate overboard?' he asked. 'Wouldn't it have had the word RUM on the label? I don't understand?'

'Neither did I, Jack. And the first thing I did was drag the crate out of the sea and have a look at what was written upon it. What I saw was:

'BOTTLES. HANDLE WITH CARE!'

Jack laughed. 'So, they thought it said *books*, but it really said *bottles*.'

'Indeed!'

'And did all the other crates come ashore then, too?'

'They did,' said Robinson. 'Fifty or more of them! All bobbing in the surf. I dragged them all on to the beach and found – well, all the things you see in my cave!'

Jack nodded. 'That was a brilliant story, Robinson – and I think it really does sound as though your pirate *was* Bad Bob.'

'I think he must have been,' said Robinson. 'And if he's as wicked as you say he is – and such a hater of beards – I'm jolly lucky to be alive! But tell me more of Old Ma Rollock, Jack. And of your family. Was your father a fisherman?'

'Oh no,' said Jack. 'We didn't . . . we don't live in that fishing village, we went there for holidays. We used to go there for two or three days in every summer. We couldn't go more; it was a long ride to the coast and my parents couldn't spare more time. But I loved the sea. Those were the best days of the year for me.

'My father and mother were farmers; they had a farm about fifteen miles inland.'

Jack began to speak of his family and of the life he'd left behind in England. Of the woods and the hills and the grey stone farmhouse where he was born, of his mother and his father and his little sister, Molly. Of old Morgan the horse, and Minx the cat and Jummie the dog, and of playing games at Christmas time when the snow was deep on the moor and the smell of cooking goose filled the house. All the wonderful memories of his life spilled out like the tumbling waters of a babbling brook . . . until suddenly his voice became a croak, and he was unable to speak more. And he began to cry.

Robinson shuffled up beside him and put an arm around Jack's shoulders.

'But why ever did you run away?' he asked. 'Were you unhappy? It all sounds like paradise to me. You *did* run away, didn't you?'

Jack was silent for some time. Then he sniffed and nodded. 'I wish I hadn't. Oh, Robinson, what am I going to do? I *must* get back home. I can't stay here for nineteen and a half years like you; I would die of homesickness. What am I going to do?'

'Don't you worry, Jack,' said Robinson. 'You *will* get back home. Be sure of it! I may not have a boat, but I've had another idea!'

Chapter Fourteen

Robinson's Idea

'A message in a bottle?' asked Jack, as they sat on the rocks by the pool the next morning. 'Is that your idea?' He couldn't hide the disappointment in his voice. It didn't sound like much of a plan.

'Quite so!' replied Robinson. 'You write a message, pop it into a bottle, cork it up and throw it into the ocean.'

'What good will that do?'

'My dear Jack – it's like posting a letter, isn't it? Don't you see? Posting a letter requesting help. With a bit of luck, someone on a passing ship will pick up your bottle, read your message and set about searching all the local islands to rescue you.'

Jack wasn't impressed.

'But what are the chances of anyone *finding* the bottle?'

he asked. 'One little bottle in the middle of a great ocean? It sounds like a hopeless idea, Robinson!'

'Not at all, Jack, not at all. You see, you won't just send *one* bottle; you'll send lots – hundreds! Hundreds of messages requesting help! One of them is bound to be found. I have any number of empty bottles.'

Jack remembered the empty bottles outside the cave.

'There were quite a number of crates labelled 'BOTTLES. HANDLE WITH CARE!' on the *New Horizon*,' said Robinson. 'I have several years' supply yet!'

Still, Jack didn't seem convinced.

'I have paper too,' said Robinson, 'for the messages. Not blank paper, mind you, but I do have *books* – lots of them. We can tear the pages from a book and use those.'

'Books?' queried Jack. He'd seen that Robinson had one book, but where were the others?

'I have a great library of books at the back of the cave,' said Robinson. 'I can certainly spare one.'

A great library of books! What else did Robinson have in his cave?

'We can start by using the pages of *this*,' said Robinson, picking up a book from the sand. It was the one he'd been reading when Jack had first met him; the book he'd taken his name from. 'I've finished it, so you can read it now. And each page you finish reading, you can tear out and use to write a message. What do you think?'

Jack was still reluctant.

'I have a pencil for the writing,' said Robinson, thrusting a hand into his right trouser pocket and pulling out a small stub of pencil. 'Not much of it left, I know, but it still has a good few messages in it, I'm sure. And I have a bottle here too, all ready.' He indicated an empty bottle lying at his feet. 'Shall we make a start?' He held the book up for Jack to take. 'It's worth a try, isn't it, Jack? It's an excellent story. As I said, it's about a castaway on a desert island! Read the first page and then we'll get started on a message.'

Jack's cheeks flushed a little. He looked embarrassed, then cross.

'I can't,' he said in a small, tight voice.

'Can't what?'

'I can't read the first page – I can't read *any* of the pages, Robinson. I can't read!'

'Oh,' said Robinson. Then, after a pause, 'No matter; I'll teach you! It's jolly useful – reading – as I'm sure those two pirates found out! I bet Bad Bob wasn't at all pleased when he found they'd thrown *all* the crates into the sea!' He opened the book and pointed to the first line. 'What do you say, Jack? Shall we have a go?'

'But, Robinson, I don't *want* to learn to read – not *now*. I just want to get back home, and I don't think your idea is going to work! It's a stupid idea!'

He seemed close to tears again.

Robinson was silent for a moment, then said, 'I really think it's worth a try. In fact, I have a hunch about it – I'm

sure it's going to work!'

He began to read the first page of the book.

'I was born in the year 1632, in the city of York . . .'

Jack turned away, sullen. But he was listening. How could he not be, with Robinson sitting right beside him and speaking with that wonderful voice of his. And though determined *not* to be interested in the story, Jack very soon was. The hero, Robinson Crusoe, turned out to be very like himself; he too had run away to sea.

As Robinson read, he ran his finger along the lines of text, stopping to point out particular words and explain how the letters made them sound the way they did. Then, when he'd reached the bottom of the second page, he carefully tore the sheet from the book and said:

'Now you can write your first message!'

Laying the book and page aside, Robinson knelt down and using his finger, inscribed the word 'HELP' in the sand at their feet.

'That says *HELP*,' he told Jack. 'A nice simple message to start with. Copy it on the page.'

Jack shrugged. He had little faith in Robinson's plan, but what had he got to lose? With a sigh, he picked up the book and rested it on his knees, laying the page on top of it. Then, taking the stub of pencil from Robinson, he began to copy out the word 'HELP'.

Not being a reader, he'd never learned to write, of course, but even so, his message wasn't bad:

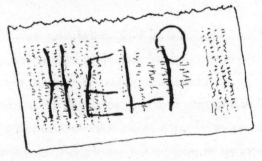

'Excellent,' declared Robinson. 'Now, roll it up and slide it into the bottle, then push the cork back in.'

A short time later Jack waded into the sea and hurled the bottle out as far as he could, watching as it spun across the sky and plopped down beyond the breakers. Gradually it was carried away by the tide until all he and Robinson could see was a tiny glassy glint, bobbing among the waves.

And then it was gone, lost to the limitless ocean.

Chapter Fifteen

Books

'What's that?' asked Jack, pointing across the cave. Robinson had just picked something out of a small bowl on top of a chest of drawers covered with clutter.

'This? Why, this is my needle!' he declared, holding the little object up with pride. 'One of the most precious and important things in the whole cave – a marvellous invention! Where would mankind be without it? One could almost say it is the *germ* of civilization – the beginning of proper clothes! The–'

'I didn't mean that,' interrupted Jack. The needle may have been interesting to Robinson, but it wasn't to Jack. 'Sorry, I meant the glass jar beside the bowl – what's inside it?'

Something had caught his eye.

'Oh,' said Robinson, a little deflated. He put aside his needle and picked up the jar. 'In here is something very curious,' he said, tipping the jar's contents into the palm of his hand. Jack walked over to look at what Robinson was holding. He saw ten tiny tortoise shells, no larger than his fingernail.

'I found one too!' cried Jack, excitedly.

Earlier that day he'd picked up just such a tortoise shell from the sand near the beach and was struck by what a peculiar contrast it was to the living giant tortoise. He took the shell from his pocket and held it up for Robinson to see.

'Are they babies, do you think?' he asked. 'Babies that never got to grow big like Caliban?'

'You'd think so, wouldn't you?' said Robinson. 'But actually, they're far too small to be giant tortoise babies. And if you look at them closely, Jack, you'll see that they're not babies at all.'

Jack examined the shell he was holding.

'That's odd,' he said. 'It looks like an *old* tortoise shell – all scratched and gnarly like Caliban's shell – not a new baby one.'

'Exactly, Jack. I think these *were* old tortoises. I think there must have been a colony of midget tortoises on this island, as well as giant ones like Caliban.'

'Are there any left?'

Robinson shook his head. 'I don't think so. At least, I've never found any live ones; only empty shells. And here's another odd thing: I've only ever found these tiny tortoise shells – never any giant ones. There must surely have been other giant tortoises, besides Caliban, but what became of them is a mystery.'

Jack pondered this for a moment. 'Perhaps they were taken away – off the island, I mean – by sailors, who killed them for meat?'

Robinson nodded. 'Yes, you're probably right. I expect that must be the answer, and that might also explain Caliban's loathing for humanity!'

He poured the tiny tortoise shells back into the jar and replaced it on top of the chest of drawers.

'Anyway, I was going to suggest I stitch up those tears in your shirt before supper. But before I do that, I'd like to show you something else!'

He picked up a lantern and, lighting it using the tinder-box, led Jack into the darkness right at the back of the cave. They passed down a kind of narrow corridor until a larger chamber opened around them and their shadows loomed high against the rock walls. Ahead, Jack saw numerous winking sparks of light, and for a brief unsettling moment, thought they were eyes. But the lantern soon revealed them to be bottles; hundreds of them.

'My rum cellar!' declared Robinson. 'But that's not what I want to show you.'

A little further in, Jack saw a pile of books, rising almost as tall as Robinson. Then another, and another, and as Robinson swung the lantern from one side to the other, Jack saw that there were hundreds of piles of books, all around them and stretching back into the darkness.

'My great library of books!' said Robinson.

Jack had never seen so many books, nor dreamed there could ever be so many – not even in the whole world.

'Wonderful, don't you think?' said Robinson with obvious pride.

Jack nodded vaguely, but it was really their quantity that impressed him.

'There are books here on every subject,' said Robinson. 'Books of history, of science, of medicine and philosophy, atlases and almanacs, books of geography, geometry and mathematics. Why, *all* the knowledge and wisdom of mankind must be here in this library, Jack! At least, the wisdom of all those who wrote in books. And there are stories, too – fantastic stories, beautiful stories – many of the greatest stories ever written are *here*. The whole world is here!'

Robinson's voice thrilled with passion as he made this little speech, and Jack was suddenly moved – exhilarated. His imagination was stirred in a way it rarely had been before, and certainly never by *books*. But when Robinson fell silent Jack's excitement quickly faded.

'It's not though, is it?' he said with a shrug. 'The world, I mean. It's out there and all around us. They're just books.'

Robinson sighed, deflated. He shook his head. 'You think that now, Jack, but when you've learned to read, you'll understand; you'll see that they are far more than *just* books. They have the power to enchant and cast spells just as powerfully as any magic potion!'

Jack frowned, confused. 'How?' he asked.

Robinson reached over and picked up a book from the pile beside him.

'This very book,' he said, 'drew me to this island as irresistibly as the moon draws the tides! It is a play by a man named William Shakespeare, called *The Tempest* – the story of another castaway, in fact, whose name is Prospero. I once heard an actor from a troupe of travelling players recite a short speech from this play in a town square. He spoke of spirits melting into thin air, and of visions of cloud-capped towers and gorgeous palaces and solemn temples, of the great globe and all those upon it fading like mist in the air, and he ended with: "We are such stuff as dreams are made on, and our little life is rounded with a sleep . . ."

'Now, he may have just been a very good actor, but

this speech had a profound effect upon me, and I rather think that it was Shakespeare's words that struck me. They seemed to conjure visions in my imagination, and though I wasn't much of a reader then, they stayed with me, not all of them perhaps, but certainly the *feeling* they inspired. It occurred to me then that books might contain treasure just as valuable as any pirate's chest.

'Some time later, wandering the world, lost and without a home, I crept in through the broken window of a warehouse one rainy night, looking for somewhere dry to sleep. The warehouse was on the quay of a dock and was filled with packing crates. In the morning I found that the crate beside me was labelled "*Books*", and there came upon me an irresistible urge to look inside it. I found an iron crowbar in a corner of the warehouse and in a few moments had opened the crate. It was filled with brown-paper packages. I picked one up and unwrapped it. You may imagine my surprise when, inside the package, I found William Shakespeare's *The Tempest*!

'At that moment some dock workers came into the warehouse and began moving the crates. I had no wish to be caught thieving, so returned the book and replaced the lid of the crate before climbing out of the window. But still, I loitered about the dock and watched as the crates were loaded on to a ship moored there. The ship was called the *New Horizon*. This name, along with finding that book, seemed to me a very good omen. And that is why I stowed away on that ship.'

Robinson turned and walked back the way they had come, taking the book with him.

'After supper, when I've finished stitching up your shirt, Jack, I'll read you this play,' he said.

And he did. In fact, he *acted* it out, playing all the various parts himself, and he was an excellent actor. Jack laughed and thrilled and shuddered with every twist and turn of the plot.

'So that's where *Caliban* comes from,' said Jack, when Robinson took his last bow. 'You took the name from Prospero's servant?'

'Indeed,' said Robinson. 'You may recall that Prospero says to him:

"Come forth, I say! there's other business for thee:
'Come, thou tortoise! when?"'

Chapter Sixteen
Stories

'Maybe it was meant to be "*sea*",' suggested Robinson, sitting on the beach the next evening.

'Sea?' asked Jack.

'The word on the piece of paper,' explained Robinson. 'Instead of "she", maybe whoever wrote it meant to write "sea"?'

Jack nodded. 'They sound nearly the same. Are they spelled nearly the same?'

'Well, not really,' admitted Robinson. 'It's an odd mistake, if it is that. I just thought it might make sense if it was part of a ship's log. The captain usually writes an entry every day, doesn't he? Noting down the ship's position – that would be the numbers at the top – and anything of interest that's happened that day. Maybe he saw something

"*On the sea*"?'

Reaching inside his pocket, Robinson took out the fragment of paper and, leaning forward, they both examined it by the light of the fire.

'I'm sure we're *not* misreading it,' he said. 'It certainly reads as *she* and not *sea*. And if it *is* part of a ship's log, the real mystery is: why was this fragment being held by the hand of a dead sailor buried in the sand of this lonely little island?'

Jack had no answer to this, but he loved a puzzle; he'd been pondering over the words on the fragment of paper ever since they'd found it.

Robinson refolded the paper and put it back in his pocket.

'All very strange and mysterious,' he said, throwing a few more branches on the fire. 'But then the world is full of inexplicable things. Indeed, I've encountered a fair number of them myself!'

He then proceeded to recount several adventures of a most curious and improbable nature, so far-fetched that Jack more than once said, 'Really? That can't be true!'

To which Robinson answered, 'It most certainly is, Jack. Every word of it!'

He'd once been a sailor, it seemed, like Jack, and in his time had sailed upon most of the world's oceans and been employed as all things from ship's cook to harpooner on a whaler. He finished with the story of how he'd once caught a very large shark with a mop.

Jack thought Robinson's stories were wonderful. And he loved listening to the sound of Robinson's voice; he could have listened to it all night had not Robinson insisted they retire to bed soon after the sun had set. For those first few days that Jack was on the island, the evenings on the beach with Robinson telling his marvellous stories were, perhaps more than anything else, the thing that kept him going. He was enthralled and captivated, and while he listened to Robinson, all his fears and doubts, and his desperate home-sickness were, for a while, soothed away and forgotten. Each night he slept soundly and dreamed only of the wonderful images Robinson had planted in his mind.

Chapter Seventeen
Driftwood

Every morning, as Robinson read a little more of Robinson Crusoe's story, he would encourage Jack to try some of the simpler words for himself and, day by day, Jack's reading improved.

When they'd finished, the page would be torn from the book and Jack would write a message on it and put it into a bottle, then take it down to the ocean.

One day, as he watched that day's bottle bobbing away among the waves, with the surf washing about his ankles, Jack felt something bump against his leg and, looking down, saw that the receding water had left a small piece of driftwood beached on the wet sand. He bent down and picked it up. It was about twelve inches long and was worn and weathered where the sea had eaten away at cracks and holes, yet it still retained a few flecks of paint.

His hands began to tremble.

'What have you got there?' called Robinson, standing behind him further up the beach. Jack didn't answer.

'Jack? What's up?'

Robinson walked down to see what Jack had found. The boy looked stricken – as white as a sheet.

'Boat,' he mumbled, holding up the piece of driftwood. 'My boat . . .'

Robinson understood immediately: Jack had found another piece of wreckage from his ship – the *Wessex*. The sight of it must have brought the storm back to him in all its horror. Robinson put an arm around Jack's shoulders and guided him back up the beach. Then, gently, he sat Jack down on the sand and held him, dismayed to see that tears had begun to run down Jack's cheeks.

'It's all right, Jack,' he said, in a quiet, soothing voice. 'All that's in the past, you're safe now.'

For a long time, they both sat in silence. Then, when Jack finally spoke, it was not of the storm; he seemed to be talking of a memory from long ago.

'It was my birthday,' he said, in a small, shaky voice. 'I was five. We went to the seaside in the farm cart. It was the first time I ever saw the sea – the boats on the shingle, the whitewashed cottages along the shore, the seaweed, the crabs. I found a pool among the rocks and I set it down on the water. But I didn't know about the sea then; I didn't understand. And a wave – a great wave came crashing over the rocks and into the pool and took it away and I cried out. I cried and cried, and I splashed out into the big waves, and could hear my father's voice calling my name over and over and then I was under the water, and I thought I would drown . . . but my father caught me up and took me back to the beach. And then it was too late . . . the sea had taken it . . .'

Robinson was at a loss.

'And what was it?' he asked gently.

'My boat,' replied Jack. 'The present my father had made for me, a little blue boat with red sails. It was called *The Lucky Pebble*. The sea took it, and we could only watch as the little red sails disappeared among the waves, far offshore. It was lost.'

Still Robinson did not understand, not until Jack lifted the fragment of driftwood and said:

'This is my boat.'

Chapter Eighteen
A Little Black Pebble

R obinson frowned.
      'Your boat?'

Jack nodded.

Robinson looked down at the piece of driftwood, examining it more closely. He saw that the flecks of paint were indeed blue and saw also that on one side were small stumps, which may have been the remnants of masts.

'Why, it is a boat! You're quite right, Jack, but I don't think it can be *your* boat. Think of how big the ocean is and how many islands there are in it. What are the chances of *your* boat washing ashore on this tiny island? It's just a rather similar boat, perhaps.'

Jack shook his head, then lifted the fragment towards Robinson and pointed to one end of the piece of wood.

Robinson leaned in closer and squinted at the place where Jack was pointing. On a patch of faded blue paint, written in white and only just discernible, were the words:

The Lucky Pebble.

Robinson raised his eyebrows. 'Good heavens!' he gasped. 'Perhaps it *is* your boat! But why ever is it called *The Lucky Pebble*? Odd name for a boat; pebbles usually sink, don't they?'

'I had a lucky pebble,' said Jack. 'I think my father thought with that name it might be a lucky boat. Huh!' He shook his head at the irony of this.

'You had a lucky pebble?' asked Robinson.

Jack nodded.

'And was it really a lucky pebble?'

'I used to think it was. My mother told me it was a magic pebble. She told me a story about it. I found it on the path one day; a shiny black pebble, and I showed it to her and asked if it was a jewel. She said, "No, Jack, that is something far better than a jewel. That is a little piece of *luck*. And luck is the most precious thing in the whole world!" Then she told me a story about how clever dwarfs mine for pieces of luck deep underground. They never sell it; they save it and only give it to the most important people. "Not kings and queens," she said, "Not *those* sorts of people. I mean widows' sons and orphans and brave princesses and children with wicked stepmothers; the people you find in fairy tales. They're the people who need luck, and though you

81

may not read about it in the stories, you can be sure that they all have a little piece of luck in their pockets. That's why the stories always have a happy ending! Put that little pebble in your pocket, Jack. And keep it safe!" And so, I did. It's been there ever since.'

He leaned over to the left, stuffed a hand into his right trouser pocket, and pulled out a small, shiny black pebble.

'Useless thing! What good has it ever done me? I must be the *unluckiest* boy in the whole world!' And closing his fist, he lifted his hand above his shoulder and threw the pebble across the sand, towards the ocean.

'Why ever did you do that?' cried Robinson, looking at Jack with bewilderment. He leaped to his feet and ran to where the little black pebble had landed. Then getting down on all fours, he began hunting in the sand until he'd found it.

'But, Robinson, it never really brought me any luck, did it?' argued Jack. And holding up the remnant of his boat, he added, 'And look at this – how lucky was my boat?'

Robinson shook his head in disbelief.

'Goodness me, Jack, don't you see? You were in a shipwreck, and you survived – the *only* survivor! Was that not lucky? And though you were lost at sea, alone in the vast ocean, you washed ashore on the only island for hundreds and hundreds of miles! Was that not lucky? Not much of an island, I admit; just a tiny scrap of sand and rocks, but nevertheless, an island with a pool of lovely, cool fresh water right in the middle of it! Was that not lucky? And not only that, but the island is covered in bushes bearing edible – well, sort of edible – fruit! Was *that* not lucky? Some might also add that it's quite lucky to find a not-too-unfriendly stranger living on the island to keep you company!

'And what about that little boat of yours? How can you say it was unlucky? Just think of the extraordinary voyage it's been on! I doubt any other little boat would survive such a voyage. There must have been storms and great waves crashing down upon it. And look there; do you see those marks, those deep scratches? I think a shark has bitten your little boat, Jack. Sharks will eat almost anything – that one I caught with a mop had just eaten a bucket! But this shark didn't eat your little boat. I expect the masts must have spiked it and that's how they were broken off. Anyway, *The Lucky Pebble* survived and sailed on and on through days and months and years until, finally, out of all the islands in all the oceans of the world, it's come ashore on *this* island, right at your very feet!

'Now if that's not the most *extraordinary* piece of luck you'll ever come across . . . then I'm a tomato! And I'm pretty sure I'm not one!

'It seems to me that you're the *luckiest* boy in the whole world!'

Robinson bent down, gently took hold of Jack's hand, and dropped the little pebble on to his palm.

'Pop that back in your pocket, Jack – and *keep it safe!*' he said.

Chapter Nineteen

A Pig's Dinner

'Do you *really* think it's lucky, Robinson?' asked Jack, staring at the pebble lying on his palm.

'I do!' said Robinson. 'Believe in it, Jack! And whenever the whole world seems to have turned against you, and everything seems hopeless, put your hand into your pocket and take hold of that lucky pebble, and remember that everything will turn out all right in the end.'

Jack put the stone back in his pocket.

'Your mother sounds like a very wise and sensible person, Jack,' said Robinson, 'tell me about her – and your father too. They seem like wonderful parents, and I really don't understand what could have made you want to run away to sea. Why did you, Jack?'

Jack shrugged, twisting the remnant of his boat round

and round in his hands. 'Don't know,' he said at last. 'I was stupid, I suppose. The world in Old Ma Rollock's stories seemed such a big and exciting place, and the farm was so small. Nothing different ever happened, just the same old things.' He shook his head and sighed mournfully. 'I wish I could go back to those same old things now. I miss it all so much, Robinson. I miss the smell of the kitchen – the smell of my mother's bread baking in the oven. I miss the chink of plates as my sister laid the table for tea. I miss the creak of the front door as my father came in from the fields. I miss it all so much. All those little things that seemed to mean nothing at all when I was *there*, mean everything to me now. I would give *anything* to be back home, Robinson.'

Robinson said nothing but put an arm around Jack's shoulders.

'Is there nothing *you* miss, Robinson?' asked Jack. 'Don't you ever think of your old life, before you were here, when you were young? Don't you ever wish you could go back?'

Robinson shook his head, and without a flicker of regret said, 'No. There is no one and nothing I wish to go back to. I never had a home like yours, Jack. All the happiness I have ever found in life, I have found here on this island. Anyway, you still haven't really explained why you ran away? It surely wasn't *just* Old Ma Rollock's stories?'

Jack shrugged. 'There was a row,' he said. 'They shouted and scolded me; my father was very angry. It was so unfair.' He paused and looked away. 'It wasn't, I suppose – unfair.

But I thought my little sister was their favourite. I couldn't see what was so special about being *younger* and a *girl*! And I couldn't see why *I* had to do more work around the farm. Then she learned to read, and I didn't know what was so special about *that*! While I helped my father clean the stables and milk the cows and stack the hay, *she* did nothing. Just read her book. And then she lost it and they blamed me; they said I'd taken it. And when they found a page of the book in the pigsty, they said I'd done a terrible thing, and they were *so* angry . . . And then I ran away.'

Robinson nodded, as if he understood exactly how Jack must have felt.

'And *did* you,' he asked, 'take your sister's book and feed it to the pig?'

There was a long pause before Jack answered, 'Yes.'

Chapter Twenty

Messages

As the days stretched into weeks, Jack began to settle into his new life with Robinson on the island. He yearned for his home just as strongly, but the acute ache of homesickness he'd felt in those first few days had gradually dulled.

Robinson taught him how to use the fishing spear and now, as likely as not, it was Jack who caught their supper while Robinson made the fire. Often, he would go foraging on his own too, collecting seaweed and shellfish and sometimes eggs. Little by little he came to know the island almost as intimately as Robinson.

Sometimes he would come upon Caliban, lumbering ponderously among the rocks and bushes, and feeding on yuckies. Unable to reach the fruits growing on the branches above, the tortoise was forced to eat those that had fallen to the ground. These were invariably beginning to rot, turning black and mushy. What they tasted like Jack could not imagine. The ripe fruits were bad enough, the rotten ones must have been foul.

One day, in an effort to befriend the tortoise, Jack picked some ripe yuckies and laid them on the ground before Caliban. The tortoise showed no interest whatever in the fruit; he looked at them with complete disdain, before turning away in disgust and stumbling off.

'I've tried it myself,' said Robinson when Jack told him of the encounter. 'He won't accept gifts – not from *us*. He'd rather cut off his nose to spite his face, the stubborn beast!'

Generally, Jack and Robinson kept out of the way of the tortoise, and he kept out of theirs.

Each morning, after breakfast, Jack sat by the pool with Robinson and continued to learn to read. He was soon able to sound letters and form words without thinking about it. And then to connect the words like the links of a chain to form sentences. And as this became easier, he began to discern the narrative; his words painting a picture in his mind's eye, as though he were intoning a magic spell and conjuring the story as he spoke. As indeed, he was.

And as well as learning to read, Jack was learning to write too. The messages he wrote on the pages of the book grew longer.

He began to write:

> Help, please, my name is
> Jack Bobbin, and I am a castaway
> on a small desert island.

Then Robinson taught him how to write his messages as formal letters:

> Thank you for picking up this message.
> I am a castaway on a desert island, which
> may well be somewhere close to your
> vessel. Would it be possible for you to
> have a quick look at all the local
> islands — just in case I am on one of
> them? Thank you so much, I very
> much appreciate your help.
> Yours faithfully,
> Jack Bobbin

Sometimes he included helpful descriptions:

it is a very small island and almost completely flat, and I think it is somewhere in the ⚓ Atlantic Ocean. But if you see an island with palm trees, don't bother stopping – it's the wrong one; there are no trees on this island, just thorn bushes. There is a clump of rocks in the middle and a freshwater spring too – so if you need to stock up on drinking water you are most welcome. Hoping to see you soon,
yours,
Jack Bobbin.

He was reading more than just one page at a time by now. Many more. And when he'd finished, he would carefully tear all the pages he'd read and write a message on each. Then he and Robinson would have to make several journeys down to the beach, carrying all the corked-up bottles. And as they watched them bobbing away among the waves – a whole flotilla of bottles – Robinson would cry:

'Now there's a sight to see! A fleet of messages! Who could miss that? Someone's bound to see *those*!'

But no one did. Or, if they did, they never came looking for Jack, and as the weeks passed, any hope he'd had in Robinson's message-in-a-bottle idea – which wasn't much to begin with – disappeared altogether.

'Give it time, Jack, give it time!' insisted Robinson.

And with a shrug, Jack said, 'I'll stick at it until the end of the book. If it hasn't worked by then, we'll have to think of something else.'

'All right, Jack, until the end of the book,' agreed Robinson. 'But I'm sure it *will* work.'

Sometimes, when Jack was feeling particularly pessimistic, and if Robinson was not with him, his messages took on a rather cynical tone. He might write: *'I'm sure this message will end up at the bottom of the ocean, so I don't suppose anyone will ever read it, but just in case, my name is Jack Bobbin and I'm a castaway'* etc. etc. . . . .

Finally, the day arrived when Jack reached the very last page of the book: page 241. He read it, tore it from the now empty covers, and wrote on it 'HELP', as he'd done on the very first page, then he put the message into a bottle, took the bottle down to the beach and threw it into the ocean.

He'd enjoyed the story, but wasn't sorry to reach the end of it.

'That's it,' he said to Robinson, as they watched the bottle drifting away. 'No more bottles!'

'All right,' said Robinson, 'but let's wait and see what happens, shall we? I'm sure something will!'

Something did, though not for some time.

Chapter Twenty-One

Robinson's Wardrobe

In the meantime, as weeks became months, Jack started to think differently about the island. Where once he had seen only monotony and desolation, he now found beauty and wonder. He would watch the long-legged red spiders spinning their webs among the branches of the thorn bushes, golden threads in the early sun's rays. He would study the beautiful yellow and green lizards basking on the warm rocks by the spring and the shy and secretive mice that ran around the beaches at dusk with their tails held straight up in the air. He swam in the ocean and marvelled at the beautiful fish he watched in the reef of coral. There were particular rocks he would rest upon; rocks that he came to look upon the way one might a favourite armchair. Places he would go to find shade, places he would lie in the sun. He began to feel comfortable on the island; he began to enjoy it.

This would not have been possible, of course, without the companionship of Robinson. He now understood his friend's appreciation of the island. And yet, unlike Robinson, Jack never came to look upon the place as home.

Every single day he would think about his family and the little farm where he was born, far away on the other side of the ocean. Memories of things he'd never thought of for years and years would come to him unbidden and cause him to catch his breath and start. His lip would tremble. Tears would prick the corners of his eyes.

He learned to stop these memories, to bottle them up and put them away, and think of other things.

One thing he thought about more and more was Robinson's wardrobe – and indeed all the other large pieces of furniture in the cave – and how they might be made into a raft. Could he really ask Robinson to give up all his beautiful furniture? It was asking an awful lot. He was fairly certain that Robinson would say yes without a moment's hesitation. And then, into his mind, came the image of his friend, sitting alone on a single remaining chair in an empty cave.

He couldn't ask. Not yet.

Chapter Twenty-Two
Jack's Story

One evening, after Jack had been on the island for more than a year, Robinson said:

'Your turn to tell a story tonight, Jack.'

Jack had already told Robinson all that he could remember of his adventures with friends back home in Cornwall, and about his life on the farm and his voyage on the *Wessex*, which, until the storm, had been mostly dull and uneventful. He'd also told almost all of the stories he'd heard from Old Ma Rollock, which he recalled almost word for word. He could only remember one that he'd not yet told.

'This is the story of Bad Bob and the treasure map,' he began, 'and I'll tell it exactly the way Old Ma Rollock used to.' Then, sitting up straight and putting on his best story-telling voice, Jack began:

'No eye, no leg, no hand, and no beard! Chin as smooth as a baby's bottom! As it always had been. But there was a time, long ago in Bad Bob's youth, when he had both eyes, two legs and a full set of ten fingers . . .

'At that time Bad Bob was first mate to another pirate captain called Sir Roger Hawks; known to all as Red Roger, on account of his long red hair and immense red beard.

One night, when Red Roger's ship, the *Scarlet Boar*, was anchored off a small rocky island, and the rest of the crew were either drunk or asleep, Red Roger woke Bad Bob, and the pair took the ship's boat and rowed ashore with a chest of treasure sitting on the bottom boards between them. It was Red Roger's personal treasure, which he was intending to bury somewhere on that rocky island. No doubt he needed Bad Bob to help lift the chest down into the boat and then out again once on the beach, other-wise he would certainly have gone off to bury his treasure alone. There was little trust between those pirates – and with good reason, as we shall see . . .

'What actually happened that night, no one ever found

out for certain, but in the early hours, one of the pirates on watch up on deck heard a voice *singing* from somewhere on the island. He was sure it was the voice of Bad Bob, and he was singing old sea shanties – on and on for more than an hour. He stopped just as the sun had begun to rise, and a little later the rowing boat was seen returning to the ship. But just one figure was pulling at the oars: Bad Bob. There was no sign of Red Roger, and no sign of the treasure. The captain had apparently met with an "unfortunate accident"; he'd fallen overboard and drowned, according to Bad Bob. And now Bad Bob was to be their captain. None of the crew were fooled by the "unfortunate accident" story; but even so, they dared not challenge the new captain; he was a formidable figure even then – huge and enormously strong, and with a particularly vicious and cruel temperament.

'One thing the other pirates were sure of, and that was that somewhere about Bad Bob's person there must be a treasure map marking the exact spot where Red Roger's treasure had been buried.

'They were right. Stuffed into a secret pocket inside the coat Bad Bob wore morning, noon, and night, was a folded sheet of paper . . .

'That paper remained untouched for many years, while Bad Bob's career went from strength to strength. He lost a leg, a hand, and an eye; and acquired a parrot and a reputation as fearsome as any pirate that ever swashed a buckle!

'But even the most infamous of pirates fall on hard

times, and there came a year when the pirating was not what it once had been, and Bad Bob had need of Red Roger's treasure.

'The map was withdrawn from its secret pocket, unfolded, and laid on the table in the captain's cabin. Smoothing out the creases, Bad Bob leaned forward and examined it. A frown creased his brow. His eye bulged with bewilderment, then disbelief. Lord Boothby – the captain's parrot – stretched out his scrawny neck to look at the map and squawked in surprise. And then Bad Bob howled in anger. A howl so loud, a shiver of vibration was sent through the whole ship, and all those on board jumped several inches into the air.

'Whatever was on that map?

'Well, only Bad Bob knew the answer to that, and he never showed the map to another soul.

'He took to pacing up and down the deck for hour upon hour, wooden leg knocking out a steady rhythm like the ominous tick-tocking of a giant grandfather clock. The other pirates kept well out of Bad Bob's way.

'From time to time, the captain would extract from his secret pocket what the other pirates assumed must be the map, and scowl at it, muttering angrily, like a bubbling, spluttering kettle. Then the knock, knock, knocking of that wooden leg would begin again.

'What was it that Bad Bob was muttering?

'Well, obviously, none of the pirates dared get near

enough to hear for themselves, but there was *someone* who could hear those angry grumblings. The parrot. Lord Boothby, sitting on Bad Bob's shoulder, could hear every word the captain said and, as everybody knows, parrots quickly learn to mimic their masters.

'And so, along with all his other unpleasant little observations, Lord Boothby took to squawking: *"The Isle of the Four Toys! The Isle of the Four Toys! The Isle of the Four Toys!"*

'And though the pirates rarely took much notice of the parrot, they took notice of this, for they knew that the parrot must be repeating Black Bob's words. They had never heard of the Isle of the Four Toys, but, quite logically, they reasoned that it must be the name of that little rocky island where Red Roger's treasure was buried. But why the map should cause Bad Bob to pace the deck muttering that name incessantly, they had no idea.

'Naturally, they were all itching to get a look at the map. But still, no one dared go anywhere near Bad Bob, nor dared *ask* the captain about it.

'However, they *did* eventually find out what was on that map, and this is how it happened.

'One day, quite by chance, one of the pirates happened to be up in the rigging, just above the spot where Bad Bob stopped pacing and took out the map to examine it. Looking down, the pirate caught a glimpse of the map – *more* than a glimpse, a proper look . . .

'Across the top of the sheet, he could see a line of words, and though he couldn't read, he guessed they must be the name of the island. Below them the paper was – *a perfect and absolute blank*!

'There was nothing there at all!

'No wonder Bad Bob had howled in anger when first taking out the "map". No wonder he paced the deck muttering angrily.

'The other pirates now quite understood their captain's exasperation – he must have taken the "map" from Red Roger's dead hand and put it in his pocket without actually looking at it. If he had, he'd have seen that Red Roger hadn't actually drawn a map!

'But why Bad Bob repeated the name of the island over and over as if it held some unfathomable secret, they did not understand.

'They could, however, now guess what might have happened that night on the Isle of the Four Toys. The old captain must have dragged his treasure chest off into the interior of the island to bury it alone, leaving his first mate on the beach with the boat, singing sea shanties to pass the time. Then he must have sat down to make a map for future reference, indicating where the treasure was buried. Bad Bob must have spied upon him and, thinking the map complete, murdered Red Roger, taken the map, and stuffed it into the secret pocket.

'Foolish pirate – Red Roger hadn't even *begun* his map,

let alone finished it! And thus, all Bad Bob had now was a blank sheet of paper! Without the exact latitude and longitude of that little island, which only Red Roger had known, it would be almost impossible to find. Nevertheless, Bad Bob searched for years and years and years . . .' At this point Jack fell silent.

'And?' asked Robinson.

'Well, Old Ma Rollock stopped at that point and said it was getting late and she'd finish the story another time. But I never heard the ending. That's why I've never told the story before.'

'Oh dear,' sighed Robinson, dismayed. 'How disappointing! Still, it was an excellent story, and very well told, Jack. I do wish I knew the ending, though. It would have been exciting to hear if Bad Bob *had* eventually managed to find that treasure chest, and lifted the lid and found it full of Spanish do . . .'

He stopped and looked across at Jack, the firelight flickering in his widening eyes. A thought had occurred to him.

Jack stared back, his mouth open. The same thought had struck him. He thrust a hand into his pocket and took out the gold coin he'd found when they'd reburied the skeleton.

'Doubloons . . .' he said, finishing off the word left hanging upon Robinson's lips.

Chapter Twenty-Three

Red Roger's Treasure

They stared at each other across the fire, silently absorbing the possibilities of that word.

'Do you think those old bones we buried could have been *Red Roger*?' said Robinson, giving voice to the thought that had sprung into both their minds.

Jack nodded. 'Which means *this* island might be the Isle of the Four Toys.'

'Where Red Roger's treasure was buried!'

Robinson jumped to his feet and began to walk round and round the fire, almost skipping, unable to contain his excitement. 'It must be! It must be!' he cried. 'And perhaps Old Ma Rollock never finished the story because it never had a proper ending; Bad Bob never found the island and the treasure! Maybe it's still here!'

Jack was just as excited as Robinson but tried not to get too carried away.

'It might not be, Robinson,' he said. 'I mean, anyone could've died with a golden doubloon in their pocket.'

'True, true, but this *is* a small island. And there *are* lots of rocks all over it – it fits the description in your story *exactly*. But you're right, let's try and think it through, let's try and imagine what happened on that night.' He paused and sat down again, beside Jack, then continued, 'We'll assume the theory the other pirates came up with is pretty accurate – it sounds plausible; that Red Roger *did* drag the chest off by himself and bury it and . . .'

'But why didn't Bad Bob just follow him,' interrupted Jack, 'to find out where he was going to bury it?'

'Hmm . . . good point,' admitted Robinson. 'But wait a minute – the singing! That must be why he was singing. Red Roger must have *told* him to sing – must have told him to sing out at the top of his voice and not to stop, otherwise he'd know that treachery was afoot. That way he knew exactly where Bad Bob was the whole time he was burying the treasure.'

'But Bad Bob *did* stop, and treachery *was* afoot, wasn't it?'

'Yes, but by then I imagine the treasure was buried and Red Roger was sitting drawing his map at the top of the beach. Bad Bob must have said something like, "Can I leave off now, Captain? Throat's getting mighty sore," and

Red Roger must have said yes.'

Jack nodded. 'I suppose that must be right – it would explain the singing.'

'Anyway,' continued Robinson, 'we'll assume he *did* go off by himself and bury the treasure – for which he'd have needed a spade, of course, and . . .'

He stopped.

'Yes?' said Jack.

'*Spade!*' cried Robinson. 'He *did* have a spade. My spade – the spade I used to bury his bones – it was not from the cargo of the *New Horizon*; it wasn't washed ashore along with all the other things; it was already *here* on the island. I found it half-buried in the sand on the beach . . . and do you know, it was in almost the exact same place that you found his bones!'

'Golly,' gasped Jack. 'Do you think it was *his* spade?'

Robinson nodded. 'It must have been. I can see it all now – Bad Bob creeping up behind him and murdering him, and tearing the map from his dying hands. It must be the truth!'

'Except for one thing, Robinson.'

'What's that?'

'Well, it *wasn't* a map, was it? It was mostly a blank sheet of paper. So, what made Bad Bob so sure that Red Roger had finished it, when in actual fact he hadn't even started it?'

'Yes, that *is* strange.'

'And he was so sure that he had the map, he didn't even

check but stuffed it into his secret pocket and didn't look at it for years and years!'

Robinson shrugged. 'I don't suppose we'll ever know the answer to that, or what *really* happened on that night. But I'm convinced that it *was* Red Roger that we buried, and that his treasure is somewhere on this island!'

Jack nodded in agreement. 'And there is one thing we *do* know for sure.'

'What's that?'

'That Bad Bob *did* tear the map from Red Roger's dying hands. Because he didn't get all of it, did he? A little piece was left behind – and that little piece is now in your pocket!'

Robinson jumped up again and thrust a hand into the pocket of his trousers. He withdrew the fragment of paper, unfolded it, and sat down once more beside Jack. Leaning in close to the embers of the fire, they both stared at the paper . . .

What was written there hadn't changed. A record of latitude and longitude, which they now realized must be the location of the island, and below that the words 'On the she', close to the torn edge of the fragment.

They both frowned.

It still made no sense to them.

'What if we put it together with the other words – the words on Bad Bob's part of the sheet?' suggested Jack.

Robinson nodded.

'On the she The Isle of the Four Toys . . .' He shook his head. 'No, that doesn't seem to make sense.'

'What about: The Isle of the Four Toys on the she?'

'Nor that.'

'Whatever could Red Roger have meant by it?'

They sat in silence for a further minute staring at the fragment of paper before Robinson said, 'Well, we can't do anything about it tonight, and it may be that we never need to decipher the meaning of it anyway – this is a very small island; I'm sure it won't be that hard to find the buried treasure!'

Chapter Twenty-Four
The Treasure Hunt Begins

Next morning, after a hurried breakfast, they made their way down to the grave on the beach.

Robinson carried the long-handled spade – Red Roger's spade – and when they reached the mound marking the grave, he stuck it in the sand and knelt down beside the gravestone. With a sharpish stone he scratched a line through the name *BILLY BONES*, and beneath it inscribed *RED ROGER*.

'Now, if this is where he sat down to draw his map,' he said, 'I think we can safely assume that he must have walked here in a fairly direct line from the place he buried his treasure, don't you think?'

Jack nodded; this seemed a reasonable assumption.

'So, let's have a look at the ground just inland from here,' suggested Robinson.

They began to retrace Red Roger's imagined footsteps. Jack was tingling with excited anticipation, but if he'd expected to see a corner of the treasure chest sticking up from the sand when they reached the top of the beach, he was disappointed. They saw no such thing.

The ground was far less rocky here than the rest of the island, so the pirate captain would have had few problems dragging his heavy chest. But there was no way of knowing how *far* he might have dragged it.

Jack looked at the unremarkable landscape before them. It suddenly seemed absurd to think that a chest of pirate's treasure was buried there somewhere. In the broad light of day, all the exciting theories of the night before – all the certainties stimulated by the dark and inflamed by the fire-light – seemed to evaporate. How could any of it be true?

'Do you really think there's treasure buried here, Robinson?' he asked.

'Why, of course I do, Jack!' assured Robinson, catching the uncertainty in Jack's voice. 'I'm absolutely certain of it! Come on, let's go and find it!' And he marched off, spade across his shoulder, peering to left and right among the thorn bushes.

Such was his confidence that Jack's enthusiasm was somewhat restored.

'But what are we actually looking for?' he asked, following behind Robinson. 'Will the chest be visible do you think – sticking up out of the sand?'

'Oh no, I'm sure it'll be properly buried, but I'm thinking there must be something marking the spot. A rock, for
instance. How else would Red Roger have been able find
the exact place again?'

'So, are we going to dig under all the rocks?'

'Well, we could. But I'm thinking it won't be just an
ordinary rock. It'll probably have something distinctive
about it.' As he said this, he pointed to a rock shaped like a
rough-hewn pyramid – 'Like that one!'

Shifting the rock to one side, Robinson began to dig.

Jack was suddenly excited again. A flutter of hope
shivered in his stomach as Robinson heaped up the sand
on the side of the hole. They found nothing, however, and
when the hole was about three feet deep, Robinson said,
'Hmm . . . Let's try somewhere else.'

A thought occurred to Jack. 'Maybe this island wasn't really called the Isle of the Four Toys,' he said. 'Maybe only Red Roger called it that? Maybe he called it that because he found four rocks that looked like toys and used them to mark the spot where the treasure was buried?'

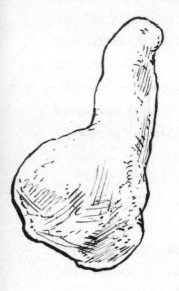

'Gosh, Jack – I think you've hit upon something there!' cried Robinson. 'That sounds very plausible, very plausible indeed! And now we have something much more tangible to search for! Let's split up, shall we? You take the area to that side, and I'll take this bit over here.'

They split up and began to look among the bushes for rocks that bore some resemblance to toys.

'What do you think – a giraffe, possibly?' called Robinson, holding up an odd-shaped rock with a long thin part jutting out. And then, 'This could be a ball, couldn't it – it's pretty round?' and, 'A rocking horse, wouldn't you say?'

None of these descriptions, however, were very convincing,

and when Robinson dug exploratory holes beneath the rocks, he found nothing.

Late in the afternoon, hot, tired and with his enthusiasm somewhat dented, Robinson exclaimed, 'Bother! I'm sure I've picked up this rock three times already! This is no good – we need a plan; we need to do the search *properly*.'

Jack was beginning to realize that though it was indeed a very small island, finding the treasure was not going to be as easy as Robinson had suggested.

'We need a map,' Jack observed. 'Then we can do a systematic search and not go over the same ground twice. I could draw it. I'm quite good at drawing.'

Back in England, Jack had often made maps; of the farm and the land all around it. And though he could not write, he'd covered his maps with little pictures of all the things he'd found exploring the countryside.

'Excellent idea!' said Robinson. 'Let's call it a day for now, we need to catch some fish before we lose the light. You can start on the map tomorrow.'

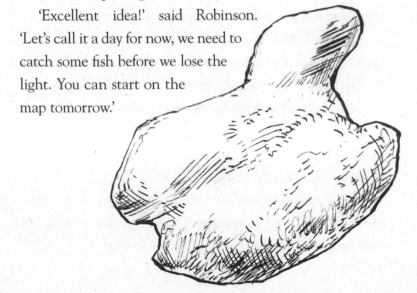

Chapter Twenty-Five

Cold Stone Cut

Next morning Robinson handed Jack a large, blank sheet of paper.

'This is the flyleaf from this atlas,' he said. 'The largest sheet I could find, and quite appropriate, I thought.'

Jack took the sheet and Robinson's pencil stub and, carrying the atlas under his arm, set off to make his map.

He started by climbing the tallest of the Skittles and roughly drawing all that he could see from there. Then he made a complete circuit of the island, filling in the details of the coastline, before walking back and forth across the island, adding all the features of the interior.

The map took him almost three days to complete and by the end of each day he was tired, scratched and bruised, but thoroughly happy. He loved to have a project.

Robinson was very impressed.

'It's beautiful,' he said, when Jack showed him the finished map. 'And I believe you have all the spellings correct too!'

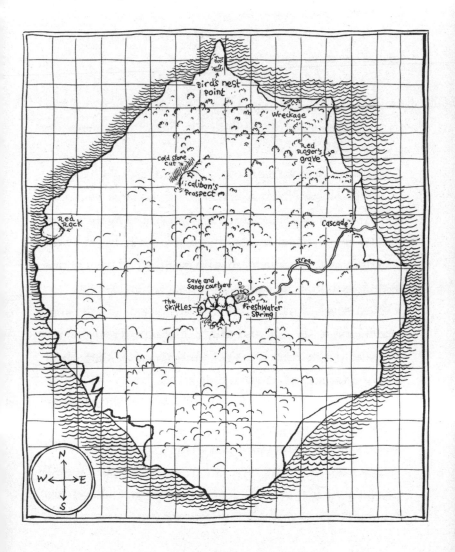

'Do you see that I've made a grid over the whole island, Robinson?' said Jack, as they looked at the map. 'I think we should search the island square by square. We'll mark out a bit of ground that's the same as one of my squares as near as we can make it, and only move on to the next one when we've searched it properly. I think we should start where we left off the other day.'

So that is where they began.

Jack marked out an area using a ball of string and four sticks that roughly corresponded to one of the squares on his map.

'This is where we'll dig today,' he said.

Robinson used the spade, which was too large for Jack to manage easily, while Jack used his hands, and by the end of the day they'd dug about twenty quite deep holes and were as certain as they could be that no treasure had been buried in that area. Jack put a cross in the square on his map.

Next day, Jack moved two of the sticks and made another square next to the first and they dug another twenty holes. Then he put another cross on his map. After three more days and three more crosses, they began to flag.

'Why ever did I think this treasure would be easily found?' said Robinson, sitting on a rock after a long and fruitless day. 'It could take us months!'

Jack looked at the five small squares he'd 'crossed' alongside all the 'uncrossed' ones. There were almost two hundred. It could, indeed, take months . . .

And it wasn't just the digging that made the treasure hunt such an onerous task. When they'd finished digging all the holes in a square, they had to fill them all in again. If they'd left them, those parts of the island would have become very difficult to walk upon and poor old Caliban would have found it impossible.

Nevertheless, they stuck at it. But as day followed day with still no sign of treasure, their passion for the hunt began to wane.

Jack remained keener than Robinson. It had become *his* project, and often he would get started early, without Robinson, who would join him an hour or two later.

It was on such a morning that he arrived alone at a place Robinson had called Caliban's Prospect; a low hillock where the tortoise was often to be found gazing out across what he clearly considered to be *his* domain. One side of this hillock dropped away sheer into a deep gully where a dark stone, about six feet by three, feet lay on the sand. The gully was like a deep gash – a cut – across the land, and the stone was always strangely cold to the touch, so Robinson had called the place Cold Stone Cut. The coolness of the stone was no doubt due to the gully being permanently in the shade, but there was there was nevertheless something about the place that gave Robinson the shivers.

Caliban, who would always seek out some shady spot in the hottest part of the day, never went down into the Cold Stone Cut.

Jack staked out his square around the hillock and the gully, and as the hillock was mostly hard rock, began to dig in the sandy bed of the gully. He felt the same way Robinson did about that place; it gave him goosebumps, and he shivered each time he thrust his hands into the cool sand. As time passed, he found himself continually looking over his shoulder, feeling sure there was someone else there with him. There wasn't, of course, but the feeling persisted and more than once he called out Robinson's name and waited for an answer. None came. The only other thing 'with him' in that narrow, sandy gully was the large, dark stone, and gradually the feeling grew upon Jack that *this* was the other presence he felt. He didn't know why, there was nothing special about the stone; it didn't resemble anything. It just seemed to be *not an ordinary stone*, and somehow Jack was both drawn to it and repelled by it. Several times he half-decided to stop digging, and to climb out of the gully and wait until Robinson arrived. But then he told himself that he was a fool and was surely overthinking things – he was just tense, excited.

It occurred to him then, that perhaps the strange feeling he felt was a kind of sixth sense that the gully was *the* place – the place where the treasure was buried.

Buried beneath the large, dark stone perhaps.

He knelt down beside the stone and was about to scoop up a handful of sand when something moved above him. Something he was more *aware* of, rather than actually

seeing. He looked up.

Someone was above him on the top of the hillock.

Caliban was staring down at him with an unmistakable look of extreme agitation. And then suddenly the tortoise was gone.

Jack frowned, then laughed. 'Why, it was Caliban! I *knew* there was somebody about. It was just Caliban!'

He lowered his eyes to the stone and dug his right hand into the sand beside it . . . and found that he had grasped another hand.

Chapter Twenty-Six

Under the Stone

A dead hand with icy cold, bony fingers.

Jack leaped up, withdrawing his hand, repulsed. Yet just for an instant, as he pulled away, he was sure that other hand had *gripped* his own.

He ran.

'Whoa! Whatever's the matter?' cried Robinson, stepping down into the gully, as Jack almost bowled him over. 'And what's up with Caliban? I've just seen him almost *scampering* away among the bushes. Never seen him move so fast!'

'*Hand!*' gasped Jack, breathing heavily, white as a sheet. 'There's . . . there's someone there – under the stone.'

Robinson put an arm around Jack's shoulders. 'Dear me, Jack, you look like you've seen a ghost. Don't worry, it'll just

118

be bones – a grave, no doubt. That other resident I spoke of who must have lived here long ago. Just bones.'

'But, Robinson, it . . . it . . .'

'What?'

Jack thought of what he was about to say. It sounded crazy. He shook his head. 'Nothing, I just got a shock.'

Robinson laid down his spade and walked up to the stone. 'Let's have a look and see who's there,' he said, kneeling in the sand.

Jack hung back, watching from the edge of the gully as Robinson carefully brushed away the sand from the place where Jack had begun to dig. A moment later Robinson frowned and sat back on his haunches. 'My, my, that's very curious. Come and look, Jack.'

Jack stepped down into the gully.

'Ugh!' he exclaimed, peering over Robinson's shoulder. 'It's . . . horrible.'

Reaching out from beneath the stone, was a hand – grasping, rigid, arched fingers clawing at the sand. Stretched upon the hand, wrinkled and mottled black, was a sheath of mummified skin and sinew.

Robinson gave a low whistle. 'Doesn't look like this person met a very pleasant end. I think we should investigate further – I think we should lift the stone.'

Jack wasn't sure he wanted to see what lay beneath the stone. 'Really?' he questioned.

Robinson ignored his reluctance and reached down

into the sand to find the edge of the stone. Gripping it, he braced his feet apart, bent his knees and with a growl of effort, lifted the stone an inch or two. Then, with a roar of exertion he heaved it up and up and up until he could flip it over completely.

It fell with a dull thump into the soft sand.

In the place where the stone had been, was a mummified figure. A few faded portions of material partially covered a body of shrivelled, parchment-like skin and shattered bones – crushed almost flat but for the arched, claw-like right hand. The skull was turned to one side, mouth open in a silent howl, splintered teeth loosened from the fractured jaw. And from the withered scalp, long grey hairs sprawled, fan-like, over the sand.

The figure was clearly the victim of some terrible accident.

Jack stared, horrified.

Robinson shook his head, appalled at the thought of what must have befallen this unfortunate figure. He looked up.

'The stone must have been balanced up there, on the top of the hillock,' he said. 'And then one day . . . it must have fallen. Just rotten bad luck that they were down here underneath it. I always knew there was something strange about this place – and that stone in particular. Places somehow retain traces of past events, I believe. A kind of "place memory". This terrible tragedy must somehow still linger

about the gully.'

Jack nodded. Robinson was probably right, but Jack couldn't help the feeling that the strangeness of the place – the disquiet and unease, which was stronger than ever now – came not so much from the tragic accident, but from the mummified figure itself. As if some malign spirit was still present in the shattered remains. He shivered, remembering the touch – the *grip* – of that claw-like hand. And looking down at the hand, he suddenly saw something in the sand below it.

'Isn't that one of those shells?' he said, pointing, but reluctant to investigate for himself. Robinson gently lifted the mummified hand and picked up a tiny tortoise shell.

'Hmm, I wonder . . .' he mused. 'Do you think it's possible that they were bending down to pick this up when the accident happened?'

'I think they might have been,' agreed Jack. 'Look there, look at that!' He was pointing at something encircling the figure's neck. A necklace of some kind. Looking closer, they saw, threaded on to a twisted length of fibre, like beads, a row of thirty or more tiny tortoise shells, some shattered, but some still intact, pressed into the sand.

'Jewellery of some sort, I suppose,' said Robinson. 'Perhaps these remains are those of a woman?'

They were both silent for some time, then Jack spotted something else.

'What's that?' he said, pointing to a dark object, partly

obscured by one of the faded patches of material. 'It looks sort of . . . *hairy*.'

Robinson bent down, lifted the flap of material and picked the thing up.

'Why, it's a book!' he declared. 'Bound in black leather that is indeed *hairy* in some places.'

When he opened the book, they both got a shock. A dreadful stench suddenly filled the air, so powerful that Robinson was obliged to close the book again very quickly. What they'd seen, in the brief moment the book had been open, was a page covered with small handwritten script and stained with dark splashes and splodges.

'It looks like a journal of some sort,' said Robinson. 'Or a diary. Though I can't imagine why it smells so awful! I think we should hang on to it; we might learn who this person was and how they came to be on this island.'

He laid the book aside, and they both looked at the mummy to see if there were any other clues to be discovered about it. They could see nothing more, however, and neither had any desire to lift up the body.

'What are we going to do with . . . with *them*?' asked Jack. 'We can't leave them like that. Are you going to put the stone back?'

'No,' replied Robinson. 'I don't think that would be very nice. I think we should bury them properly – though I'm not inclined to move this body the way we moved Red Roger's bones. I think, instead, we should bury them under a mound.'

He picked up the spade and began to pile sand on to the mummified remains, while Jack began gathering rocks. When the mound was about three feet high, they covered it with the rocks until it looked like a low cairn, such as one might find on a mountain top. Robinson then picked up a flat slab of rock and scratched upon it: *Here Lies the Collector of Tortoise Shells*', and placed it on top of the cairn.

The Curious Book

The following morning, Jack moved his sticks and string and made another square beyond the hillock and the gully, deciding to leave that square uncrossed. They would come back there when all the others had been investigated, perhaps; when the disturbing events of the day before were less fresh in his mind.

They remained fresh, however, for a long time, and seriously dampened his enthusiasm for digging. Every time he thrust his fingers into the sand, the image of that mummified claw-like hand swam before his eyes, and he seemed to feel its icy-cold grip.

Robinson was left to do the digging. Jack staked out the ground each morning and shifted all the rocks he could move, and then, at the end of the day, put a little cross on his map. They progressed very slowly.

'What do you say we do this treasure hunting every *other* day, Jack?' said Robinson, resting on his spade one evening, very tired. 'It's awfully wearisome digging *every* day!'

So, they dug for treasure only every second day.

And then only once a week.

Then it became just an occasional activity.

But even though the number of crossed squares on Jack's map increased only very slowly, they never gave up.

Caliban had remained invisible for almost a week after the finding of the mummy. Where he'd been hiding, they never found out, but something had scared him badly; they could see it in his eyes. Doubt was clearly visible there, and they would see him jerk his head nervously from side to side, as if trying to look over his shoulder. Jack felt sure that Caliban must have known about the person under the stone, and perhaps he had the same feelings about that person that Jack had.

One day they saw the tortoise laboriously climb the hillock and peer gingerly over the edge, down into the shaded gully. He remained there, looking down, for a long time before finally raising his head, seemingly satisfied.

The unpleasant-smelling book that they'd found, Robinson put away in a corner of the cave, meaning to investigate it later – when the memory of that awful smell had dulled a little, perhaps. So, it wasn't until several weeks had passed that he came upon it one day and, taking it outside and holding his nose, opened it again.

So powerful was the stench that Robinson's eyes began to water. He blinked several times before he was able to see what he was looking at. The handwriting was tiny and a lot of it indecipherable, and it was made even more illegible by the splashes and splodges that covered the page. But one thing he noticed straight away: he was looking at what seemed to be a list.

Holding his breath, he lowered his head and examined the book more closely. From what he could read, he understood it to be a list of ingredients. The book must be a collection of recipes, perhaps? And that might explain all the smears and smudges: it had been used by a very messy cook. But was it a book of recipes? The ingredients seemed to be very odd: bat's wing, tongue of snake, nightshade root, toad's eyeball . . .

Suddenly it dawned upon Robinson what the book was.

'Jack!' he called, looking up to the top of the Skittles, where Jack was sitting.

Jack looked down.

'Do you know what this book is? It's a book of magic spells! That person we found under the stone must have been a *witch*!'

Jack's mouth dropped open in surprise. But then again, he wasn't really all that surprised. This only seemed to confirm his uneasy feelings about the mummy.

Climbing down from the Skittles, he went around to

join Robinson in the courtyard.

'There's a spell here to cure warts!' said Robinson, as Jack approached, pulling a face, and holding his nose. 'And another to *give* you warts!'

Gingerly turning the pages of the curious book, they discovered spells that could make someone fall in love and others that could cause one to hate. There were spells to make one beautiful, or ugly; to cure baldness, or headaches – there was even a spell to turn someone into a *werewolf*.

'But it's all nonsense,' declared Robinson, when they finally closed the book, unable to bear the smell any longer. 'I don't believe in this kind of magic at all. It's just mumbo jumbo.'

It may have been, but nevertheless Robinson remained fascinated by the witch's spell book and continued to periodically explore its pungent pages over the next week or so. On the very last page of the book his eye was caught by the word *rum*. It was one of the ingredients for a potion. The top of the page was heavily stained, and the name of the spell was difficult to read, but the words of the incantation sounded rather like a sailor's drinking song. They went:

Rum rum yummy yum rummy rummy yummy yummy . . .
and so on and so on for line after line. Robinson began chanting this and the words soon got stuck in his head, the way catchy tunes do.

'What *is* that you keep saying?' asked Jack, after listening to Robinson muttering away for much of the day.

'What? Oh, sorry. Magic spell! Can't get it out of my head.'

But one day, Jack was startled by Robinson crying out something else entirely.

He ran out of the cave.

'What's the matter, Robinson? What did you say?'

'*Sycorax*, Jack!' said Robinson, in a voice filled with wonder. 'That was the name of that witch! I've just found it at the front of this book!'

Jack shrugged, none the wiser.

'Don't you remember who Sycorax was, Jack?'

Jack shook his head.

'Sycorax was the name of the witch in *The Tempest*! The witch who lived on the island before Prospero and Miranda were shipwrecked there!'

For a moment, Jack was silent, taking in the significance of this. Then he said:

'Do you mean Shakespeare's play was all true? And that *this* island is Prospero's island?'

Robinson shook his head. 'I don't think so, Jack. I think the play is fiction, but it may be that Shakespeare took the name and the idea of a witch being banished to an island from a real event. It may be that *our* witch is the original Sycorax! Which is pretty incredible, isn't it?'

It was. To think that the island – *their* island – had a real connection to Shakespeare's play was amazing, and for days, Robinson walked about with a perpetual smile, shaking his head and mumbling, 'And if *she* was Sycorax, that almost makes *me* Prospero. Ha! Imagine that!'

Jack spent much of his time sitting on top of the Skittles puzzling over Red Roger's 'map-that-wasn't-a-map'. He was more and more convinced that solving this puzzle would be the way to find Red Roger's treasure, and day after day he thought about the Isle of the Four Toys, and of how the island might have acquired such a name. Then, early one morning as he mumbled to himself, '*Four Toys, Four Toys, Four Toys* . . .' the words suddenly became something else . . . and all the pieces of the puzzle fell into place.

Chapter Twenty-Eight
Jack Solves the Puzzle

Jumping to his feet – and nearly falling from the rock –
Jack let out a wild yell of exultation.

Robinson, sitting on the rocks below, looked up with a
start.

'Whatever's the matter, Jack?'

'I've worked it out!' cried Jack, scrambling down and
running towards Robinson. 'I've got it! I've got the answer!
I've *solved* the mystery of the map! Come on! We must find
Caliban!'

And before Robinson had a chance to question him
further, he was gone, bounding over the rocks away to the
north.

'Caliban?' called Robinson, putting down the book he
was reading and running after Jack. 'What's Caliban got to

do with it? And where are you going?'

Jack, already fifty yards ahead, stopped briefly and called back, '*Caliban's Prospect* – that's where he usually is, isn't it?' And then he was off again.

Minutes later, he reached the mound above the gully where they'd found the mummy, but there was no sign of the tortoise. He looked east, west, north and south. Nothing.

'Why . . . ?' puffed Robinson, catching up, a little out of breath. '*Why* must we find Caliban?'

'Because he *did* finish!' answered Jack. 'He did finish writing on that piece of paper!'

'Who – Caliban?'

'No! Red Roger, of course! He hadn't drawn a map because he didn't need one – not on that paper. But he *had* finished, and he must have put away his pencil and begun to fold away the paper – and *that's* why Bad Bob thought he'd finished drawing a map!'

'So, where does Caliban come into this?'

'We got the words wrong, Robinson! The pirates had them wrong too! They must have misheard what Lord Boothby was squawking, or else the parrot misheard what Bad Bob was muttering. It wasn't *four toys* at all, it was –'

'*Tor-toise!*' exclaimed Robinson, suddenly understanding.

'Exactly!'

'Why of course it must be that! *The Isle of the Tortoise* makes much more sense!'

'But even that's not quite right, Robinson, because Bad

132

Bob wasn't actually muttering "*the* Isle of the Tortoise", he was muttering just "*Isle* of the Tortoise" – or rather what *sounded* like "*Isle* of the Tortoise". I think the pirates must have added the "*the*" when they told the tale, thinking it didn't make a difference, but it made *all* the difference!'

'Wait a minute,' said Robinson. 'If there was no "*the*" and it wasn't "*isle*" then . . . Aha!' Enlightenment had begun to dawn upon Robinson. 'Bad Bob didn't have the whole sheet of paper, of course! So, if "*isle*" was just the *end* part of that first word . . . that's probably why he was pacing up and down the deck, muttering it all the time – trying to work out what the *whole* word was!'

'Exactly!' cried Jack. Then he got down on his knees and with his finger, wrote in the sand:

LL OF THE TORTOISE

'That's what was on Bad Bob's piece of paper! Do you see? Bad Bob was muttering the sound of two *ells*, which the parrot and the other pirates mistook for the word *isle*.' He stood up, and said, 'Now, write down the words that are written on the scrap of paper in your pocket *in front* of what I've written.'

Robinson did, but it wasn't until the final 'E' that he realized the meaning of what he was looking at . . .

'On the shell of the tortoise!'

Chapter Twenty-Nine

On the shell of the tortoise

'Yes!' cried Jack. '*That's* what Red Roger wrote!'

Robinson stared at the words in the sand, awed by Jack's cleverness. 'You *are* a genius. I can't imagine how on earth you worked all that out, but it all fits, doesn't it? It all fits perfectly, and it all seems crystal clear now; it *must* be right. Except . . .' He paused and turned to see that Jack was already off searching among the bushes for Caliban.

'Jack,' he called. '*What* was on the shell of the tortoise?'

'Why, Robinson, don't you see? The *map* of course! Red Roger scratched the treasure map on Caliban's shell!'

Robinson clapped his hand to his forehead. 'Gosh – what a fool I am. Of course he did! What a clever thing to do. No one would ever think that piece of paper had anything to do with buried treasure – unless they knew about this island and old Caliban. It was brilliant. What an ingenious idea!'

'Yes, Robinson. Now let's *find* him!'

It wasn't until midday, when they returned to the fresh-water spring to quench their thirst, that they found the tortoise. He was sleeping on the sand by the pool. Kneeling down beside him, they began to scrutinize Caliban's shell.

Naturally, it bore the signs of much wear and tear; it was probably hundreds of years old. All over it, there were marks and scratches, quite apart from the natural grooves and ridges of the interlocking plates.

Jack frowned. 'Can you see anything that looks like a map?' he whispered. 'I can't. And if there *is* a map here, how do we know which scratches are part of it and which aren't?'

Robinson stood up and walked around the sleeping tortoise, looking at the shell from all sides. He sighed and shook his head 'No, I can't see anything that looks like a map there either.'

Jack was crestfallen. 'So, there's no map then! I was so sure my theory was right.'

Robinson said nothing but closed his eyes and began to stroke his beard.

'Aha!' he exclaimed after a minute or so. 'There's one thing we've forgotten to account for, Jack.'

'What?'

'Time!'

'Time?'

'Indeed! Time. It might be thirty or forty years since Red Roger buried his treasure, and the shell of a tortoise – like the rest of the animal – *grows*. This shell has changed somewhat since the time Red Roger scratched his map on it.'

'So, there *was* a map, but now it's lost?'

'Not at all, Jack – it's just been *rearranged* a little.'

'What do you mean?'

'Well, as I understand it – and I know a little about this; I've read a book – the plates that make up the tortoise's shell, *scutes* I think they're called, grow in layers; newer, larger layers forming below existing scutes and making growth rings, like in the trunks of trees. The layers that

Red Roger scratched his map on have partly been worn away but have also become separated by all the newer layers that have grown up underneath them. So, what remains of the map – and I'm sure there must be traces of it here – has become fractured into several parts which have moved further and further away from each other over the years. Do you understand?'

'I think so,' said Jack. 'But if that's so, the map will be impossible to find!'

'Not so, Jack, not so. We just need to know where to start looking. I think what we need to find is . . . Ah ha! Look there!' He put his finger on a spot almost at the apex of Caliban's shell.

Jack leaned in close and saw, just beside the end of Robinson's finger, a small scratched 'x'.

'*That* is where the treasure is buried!' declared Robinson.

Jack shrugged. 'Maybe it is, Robinson, but that's no help to us without the rest of the map.'

'Oh, the rest of it will be there, Jack – or traces of it at least – we just have to find it. Now, pop back into the cave and fetch *your* map, and bring out a few blank pages from the books, if you can find any – and the pencil, too.'

Jack ran back to the cave and returned a few minutes later with the map, some blank pages, a book to lean on, and the pencil.

'Excellent!' declared Robinson. 'Now, I've been study- ing the area around that "x" and I've already spotted a few promising scratches, so what you need to do is draw that part of the shell – the pattern of the scutes and all the marks and scratches on them – as accurately as you can.'

Jack sat down on a rock close to where Caliban was sleeping, rested the paper and book on his knee and did as Robinson had said.

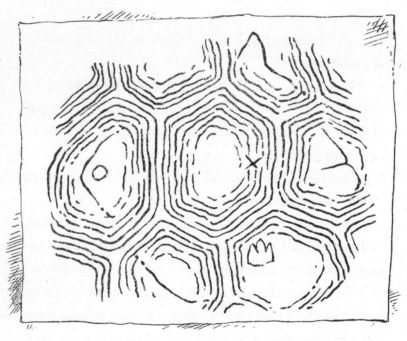

Just as he finished and handed the drawing to Robinson, Caliban opened an eye and was surprised, and not at all pleased, to see Jack and Robinson staring at his shell. He raised himself from the sand and marched off as hastily as he could. Jack got up to follow, but Robinson remained sitting, looking at the drawing intently.

'Aren't we going after him?' asked Jack.

'No need – we have your drawing now. The map must be scratched on the topmost layer of the scutes – the oldest layer. Do you see? Here, here, here and here.' He pointed to various parts of Jack's drawing. 'Draw over those lines a bit more strongly and then copy just the dark bits on a new sheet, but closer to each other. Try and make them all join together, if you can.'

Jack did and then handed the new drawing to Robinson.

'And there we have it!' exclaimed Robinson, exultant. 'Red Roger's treasure map!'

The lines Jack had drawn did indeed seem to vaguely follow the shape of the island, Jack could see that now, and there was clearly an 'x' in the middle of it, but he couldn't see that it would be much help to them.

'But it's such a crude map, Robinson. That "x" could be almost anywhere. I mean, Red Roger must have made the map very quickly, and probably by the light of the moon, and I imagine Caliban didn't lie still while he was doing it – he must have got up and tried to get away. I don't see how it helps.'

'Really, Jack?' said Robinson, shaking his head. 'I think that clever old pirate knew exactly what he was doing and has marked where the treasure is very precisely.'

'Has he?'

'Indeed. He has indicated certain landmarks on the map, do you see? That lump on the western side must surely be the Red Rock, and that, on the eastern side, is without doubt where the stream tumbles down on to the beach. Bird's Nest Point is that promontory to the north and those marks there are most certainly the Skittles. Now, if one imagines a line running from east to west between the cascade and the Red Rock' – Robinson took the pencil and carefully drew just such a line on the map – 'and another running north to south between Bird's Nest Point and the Skittles.' He drew another line. 'Where do the lines intersect?'

'At the "x"!'

'Exactly, Jack!'

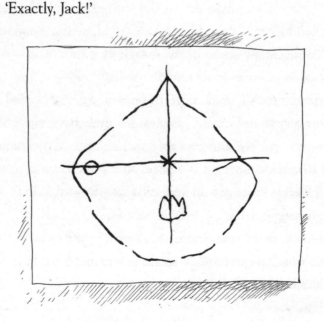

Chapter Thirty
Digging For Treasure

Ten minutes later they were standing on a small patch of sand entirely surrounded by very dense, quite tall, thorn bushes. They'd torn their clothes and scratched themselves quite badly getting to this spot, and now Robinson was peering over the bushes to north, south, east and west. He stepped a few paces to the left, looked again, then stepped forward and looked once more, aligning his position exactly between Bird's Nest Point, the Skittles, the Red Rock, and the Cascade.

Satisfied, he thrust his spade down into the sand and declared:

'This is the spot!'

Then he began to dig.

Jack could barely contain his excitement. His heart was

racing, and each time Robinson put his foot to the spade and drove it into the sand, he expected it to hit something solid. Yet time and time again, the blade slid smoothly into the unresisting sand and struck nothing. As the hole grew deeper and the pile of sand beside Robinson grew taller and taller, an unwelcome whisper of doubt began nagging at the back of Jack's mind. After ten minutes or so, Robinson began widening the hole, just in case his alignment – or indeed, Red Roger's – had been a little out, and after another ten minutes, he was standing in a hole three feet deep and almost six feet in diameter. Yet still, he'd found no trace of any treasure chest.

Jack unconsciously put his hand into his pocket to hold the gold doubloon. His fingers found something else too. The lucky pebble. He took it out and holding it tightly, silently pleaded: *Oh please, please, please, if ever you were lucky, bring us some luck now!*

But still, though the hole grew deeper and deeper, the spade struck nothing more than the sand.

'Oh, Robinson,' said Jack, with a hint of panic in his voice, 'it's not here, is it? Surely Red Roger wouldn't have buried it as deep as this?'

He didn't think he could bear it if it all came to nothing – if the whole thing was just a crazy story, an invention of his imagination to fit the very few *real* facts they had discovered. Perhaps none of it was true? Perhaps there wasn't any buried treasure?

Robinson was still digging in earnest.

'Does seem deep,' he grunted, as he heaved up another spadeful of sand and tossed it back over his shoulder. 'And I suppose . . .' he thrust the blade down into the bottom of the hole once more . . . 'there's a chance . . .' up came another load of sand . . . 'someone's already been and dug it up!'

'Oh, Robinson, don't say *that*!' cried Jack in desperation. '*Who* could have dug it up, and how would they have known where it was?'

'Don't know,' panted Robinson, pausing and taking a breather, his hands resting on top of the spade handle. 'I don't say it's likely, but it's a possibility.'

Jack groaned. Despite what he said, Robinson's tone seemed to suggest it was more than a possibility. Jack was suddenly sure that someone *had* dug up the treasure. He was utterly crestfallen.

Then Robinson straightened up, his eyes brightening as an idea occurred to him.

'On the other hand,' he said, 'perhaps Red Roger *didn't* bury the treasure this deep!'

'What do you mean?' asked Jack, his heart jumping a little as he caught the note of optimism in Robinson's voice.

'I mean, perhaps the treasure chest has *become* deeper over the years!'

Jack looked blank; he didn't understand.

'How?'

'I don't mean it's sunk deeper into the sand – I don't think that's possible – but maybe more and more sand has piled up on top of it. Sand shifts, doesn't it? And it's been a long, long time since the treasure was buried. Perhaps all these bushes weren't here then, perhaps the ground was several feet lower?'

'Yes!' cried Jack, eagerly. 'That's what *must* have happened! We just have to keep digging!'

Robinson put his foot on the shoulder of the spade and pushed it into the sand once more . . .

Thud.

It hit something solid.

Jack's chest tightened; suddenly he could hardly breathe.

'Ah ha!' exclaimed Robinson, trying to keep his voice as calm as he could, though *his* hands were shaking a little. 'There *is* something here!'

Jack jumped down into the hole.

Robinson prodded the sand several more times.

Thud, thud, thud.

He stepped back and laid down the spade.

'Your turn now, Jack,' he said. 'I think *you* should be the one to investigate further. It's your treasure hunt – at least, you've done all the brainwork, I've just done a bit of digging!'

Jack knelt down, and with trembling hands, began to scoop sand away from the spot where the spade had struck something solid. In just a few moments he had uncovered a patch of dark wood with a band of rusted iron running across it.

'That looks promising!' exclaimed Robinson, bending over Jack's shoulder.

Jack continued to scoop until the domed wooden lid of what could only be an iron-bound chest was revealed. With mounting excitement, he dug and dug until the whole of the chest was uncovered.

Robinson gave a whistle.

'Whoa! Now if that isn't a proper pirate's treasure chest,

well . . . I'm a tomato!'

Jack laughed.

They had *found* it. It *wasn't* just a crazy story – it wasn't just an invention of his imagination. It was real.

The chest wasn't enormous; about thirty inches by fifteen and about twenty inches deep. Three riveted bands of iron ran across the domed top and three more encircled the rest of it. An iron handle was bolted to each of the shorter sides and an iron latch, secured by a large padlock, held the lid in place.

Jack grabbed one of the handles and tried to lift the chest. It was solid and immoveable.

So, it wasn't empty!

Robinson knelt beside Jack and began to examine the padlock.

'I'm guessing Bad Bob has the key,' he said. 'He no doubt took it after murdering Red Roger. Still, this lock is so rusted up, it probably wouldn't work anyway. Let's see if we can't smash it off.'

'I'll get a rock,' said Jack, jumping up and scrambling out of the hole.

A moment later he jumped back in clutching a rock with both hands. He handed it to Robinson, who raised it high above his head, then brought it down on the padlock with all his might – *SMASH!*

The rusty padlock broke asunder and fell away from the latch.

'Excellent!' said Robinson, smiling broadly. 'Now, Jack, do you want to have a look inside?'

With heart pounding and hands shaking, Jack took a deep breath to try and calm his buzzing nerves. He lifted the latch, gripped the two front corners of the lid, and had just begun to lift it when an unwelcome voice inside his head said: *What if it's just full of sand or rocks?*

It wasn't.

Chapter Thirty-One
Doubloons!

G old!
Pirate's gold! Shimmering – brilliant in the afternoon sun, reflecting a golden glow of joy into Jack's face and a flash of wonder and elation into his glistening eyes.

'My, my!' cried Robinson. 'You found it, Jack! You really found it!'

The chest was brimfull of Spanish doubloons.

Jack grabbed two handfuls of the coins, lifted them, and let them drop, clinking back into the chest. Then he jumped to his feet, climbed out of the hole, and began to dance around it.

'Yippee!' he cried. 'Hurrah! Hurrah! Hurrah!'

Robinson jumped up and cheered and skipped along behind him.

So loud was the sound of their rejoicing, it roused the gulls nesting on the northern promontory, who rose into the air, adding their voices to the clamour.

Then, a moment later, the thorn bushes to the right of the hole parted and an ancient reptilian head appeared.

Caliban looked up at Jack and Robinson capering about the chest of gold, and slowly began to shake his head from side to side. Jack stopped dancing when he caught sight of the tortoise. Then Robinson too, stopped. They both suddenly felt a little foolish under Caliban's penetrating gaze. Then Robinson let out a whoop of defiance and cried:

'Who cares what grumpy old *Caliban* thinks! What does *he* know – tortoises have no use for gold!' And he began to caper once more, singing a sea shanty he'd made up on the spot:

'At the bottom of a hole we found a dead man's chest,
Yo-ho-ho, I'll drink a bottle of rum!
At a spot 'tween north, east, south and west,
Yo-ho-ho, another bottle of rum!'
And so on and so on.

Jack joined in with the song and they both sang louder and louder and danced faster and faster until, dizzy and out of breath, they collapsed in a heap and lay on the sand laughing.

With a last shake of his head, an utterly unimpressed Caliban turned away and disappeared.

'We ought to be saving our breath for carrying that chest,' said Robinson, still panting. 'Come on, let's try and lift it.'

He got up, jumped down into the hole, and took hold of one of the handles. Jack took the other, and though he huffed and puffed and strained with all his might, it was really Robinson who dragged and lifted the chest up and out of the hole.

It took them almost half an hour to get it back to the sandy courtyard outside the cave, and when they finally rested, exhausted, they were both more than a little in awe of old Red Roger. He must have been an enormously strong man.

Jack opened the lid of the chest and began counting the doubloons, taking them out and dropping them on the sand as he did so.

'You're rich now, Jack!' declared Robinson as he sat and watched. 'Just think what you'll be able to do with all that gold when you get back to England!'

Jack frowned and closed his eyes for a second, mumbling, 'Twenty-five, twenty-five, twenty-five . . .'

'Sorry, didn't mean to interrupt,' said Robinson.

'It's all right. But only half of the gold is mine, Robinson. Half is yours.'

'Nonsense, Jack – you must take it all. I've no need of it.'

'But . . .'

'No, really – you must. It's no good to me! I've as much need of gold as . . . well, a *tortoise*!'

Jack laughed. Robinson was right; what use would gold be on a desert island? He resumed his counting.

It took him almost an hour to count the doubloons and when, finally, the chest was empty, the sand all around it was covered with gold. Jack had counted four thousand, five hundred and eighty-two Spanish doubloons. How much that was in English money, he had no idea, but it must be an awful lot. It *looked* like an awful lot of money; a great carpet of gold, shining in the sun. He put his hand into his pocket and took out the doubloon they'd found with Red Roger's bones. He was going to drop it down among the others, but then decided he wouldn't, and put it back into his pocket. As he did, he took hold of the lucky pebble and silently whispered, 'Thank you!'

That evening, sitting by the fire, Robinson asked, 'What

151

will you buy with your pirate's treasure, Jack?'

Jack tried to think. There was really only one thing he wanted; to get back home to England, and he would have given all the treasure, without a moment's hesitation, to a ship's captain who could take him there, he told Robinson.

'But you've enough to buy a passage home many times over, Jack,' said Robinson. 'There must be other things you'll wish to buy?'

Jack thought again. All the things he might have desired in the past seemed unimportant now. Then at last he said, 'Thatch. I'd buy some new thatch.'

'Thatch?'

'For the roof. It's leaky, and my father was always complaining about the cost of repairing it. And I'd buy a new cart for the farm, and a new dress for my mother and a hat, too. And I'd buy a whole shelf full of books for my little sister – and *I* could read them too now.'

Robinson smiled.

Chapter Thirty-Two
A Reply

Jack went to bed that night filled with the warm glow of contentment that comes when a seemingly impossible task had been accomplished. But the next morning he was in an altogether different mood. He'd woken early, before the sun had risen and, getting out of bed, he went outside and climbed the tallest of the Skittles; he knew all the footholds in the dark now. There, he sat down and faced the east, watching as the first rays of the rising sun caught the topmost branches of the thorn bushes and picked out rocks with an orange glow.

He was still there an hour or so later when Robinson came out to drink from the pool.

'What's up?' called Robinson when he saw Jack sitting on the rocks above. It was unusual for Jack to be up before him.

Jack did not answer, nor did he look down.

'I'll come up and join you,' said Robinson. Still, Jack made no sign that he'd heard him. Robinson began to climb the rocks.

Two minutes later he sat down beside Jack and began making small talk about the delicious smell of the fresh morning air, and about the fine view of the ocean and the beautiful colours in the sky. Jack remained silent.

'What's the matter, Jack?' asked Robinson at length. 'What's happened? You should be happy. You're rich! You'll be a person of some note back in England . . .'

Then Jack blurted:

'But that's just *it*, isn't it? Don't you see? *Back in England! Back in England!* I'll *never* be back in England! What use is being rich when you're stuck on a desert island for the rest of your life? What was the *point* of the treasure hunt? It was all a waste of time!'

Blinking away angry tears, he stood up and began to climb down from the rock.

Robinson remained where he was, watching as Jack stomped off into the thorn bushes.

An overwhelming homesickness had come upon Jack the moment he'd awoken that morning. Sitting on top of the Skittles, he'd looked to the east and the rising sun, where, far away across the ocean, he knew that England lay, and his mother and father and little sister, and the grey stone farmhouse where he was born and all the green fields of Cornwall and the tumbling streams and the moors and everything that was dear to him. All of it more valuable than all the pirate gold in the whole world.

All the things he'd lost.

He realized now that the treasure hunt had merely been a distraction, filling his mind and blocking out everything else. But now the gold was found, and the puzzle solved, all his desperate longing came flooding back to engulf him.

What was he to do? What *could* he do?

Two long years had passed since Jack had washed ashore among the wreckage of the *Wessex*. He was two years older, two inches taller and a good deal wiser. But he was still the same boy who'd thought himself the loneliest in all the world. He didn't think he could bear it much longer.

Sitting on the beach, arms wrapped around his shins and chin resting upon his knees, Jack was overcome with misery. He began to cry, and for many minutes, tears streamed down his cheeks, running down his legs and soaking away into the sand at his feet. Then, as suddenly as he'd started, he stopped crying, sniffed, wiped his sleeves across his eyes, and stood up.

It was no use waiting to be rescued. He must *do* something: now was the time to ask Robinson about turning all his wonderful furniture into a *raft*.

Filled with fresh resolve, Jack was about to march back to the cave when he caught sight of something bobbing among the breakers, sparkling in the rays of the early morning sun.

It was a bottle.

A bottle!

Jack was at a loss. Was someone *else* sending messages?

He ran down the beach and splashed into the water. But before he reached the bottle, the answer dawned upon him like a cold slap in the face from one of the waves: it must be one of *his* bottles. The first bottle he'd sent perhaps, with that first plaintive 'HELP' written on the first page of the Robinson Crusoe story inside it. For all of two years the bottle must have been drifting around and around the island, and now it was being washed ashore again. No doubt all the others would follow!

So much for Robinson's conviction!

Jack was suddenly angry. What a waste of time all that message writing had been! He almost burst into tears again and was half inclined to leave the bottle, so exasperated was he. It was as disappointing as a letter returned unopened; *more* disappointing; it was a crushing rejection.

However, he did pick it up.

And he found it was *not* one of his . . .

He stared at it dumbly for some moments. There *was* what appeared to be a message inside it, but it was not a page torn from a book, but a roll of writing paper tied up with a bright red ribbon.

Somebody else *was* sending messages.

Jack waded out of the ocean and walked back up the beach and sat down. He uncorked the bottle and, turning it upside down, shook it until the roll of paper dropped out on to the sand. He picked it up, untied the ribbon and began to unroll it. But before he'd unrolled more than a few inches, he yelped in surprise.

At the top of the page was an address:

Periwinkle Cottage,
Crab Cove,
Cornwall,
England

He *knew* that address!

Crab Cove was the place where he had first seen the ocean. The place where he'd lost his boat, *The Lucky Pebble*.

And Periwinkle Cottage was where Old Ma Rollock lived!

He was flabbergasted – had Old Ma Rollock written this message?

He unrolled the page a little more and read the words:

Dear Jack Bobbin . . .

Chapter Thirty-Three
Yummi Deliciosum

After watching Jack stomp off through the bushes, Robinson climbed down from the Skittles and, picking a yucky from a thorn bush beside the pool, he went back into the cave. Lying on a table was a large red book he'd brought out from the back of the cave the day before while Jack was counting doubloons. The book was called *A Comprehensive Description of the Fruits of The Tropics*, and Robinson couldn't remember ever seeing it before. He'd discovered that it was filled with beautiful full-page coloured plates, each describing a selection of tropical fruits.

It had occurred to him that he might discover the true name of the yucky in the book.

Flicking through the pages, he soon found what he was looking for: a picture of the exact same fruit he was holding

in his hand. Beneath it was the label: Fig. 8. He turned to
the facing page where the text described each of the fruits:

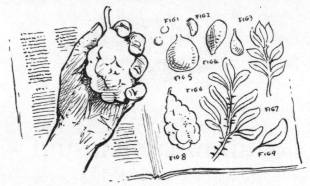

Yummy fruit? thought Robinson, that couldn't be right!
That's absurd! It must surely be a misprint. It must really be
yucky fruit, just as Jack had named it!

But it was not a misprint. And reading on, Robinson
discovered that – 'The yummy fruit, *Yummi deliciosum*, was
much prized for its delicious taste and often compared to
the food of the gods and called the Ambrosia Fruit . . .'

With increasing incredulity, Robinson read on:

'The yummy bush once grew abundantly on just a few
islands in the tropics, and though many attempts were
made to cultivate it in other places, all failed. Owing to
over-cropping, the bush died out on the few islands where it
was found and has not been known of for many years.

'The fruits when ripe were a vivid lime-green colour and
extremely unpleasant tasting but, as they overripened and
then began to rot, the taste improved dramatically. The
more putrescent the fruit, the more delicious the taste.

Connoisseurs enjoyed the yummies best as a blackened, liquefying sludge, scooped up with a spoon . . .'

Robinson burst out laughing.

'What a fool I've been!' he cried out. 'I've been eating those horrible things for twenty-one years, and for all that time I could have been eating the food of the gods! And Caliban – wise and sensible Caliban – no wonder he returned our pitying glances with such disdain!'

Robinson turned back to the book . . .

'Besides its wonderful taste the fruit was valued for other properties also. Some islanders attributed supernatural qualities to the fruit, and it was used in the making of magic potions . . .'

Suddenly, something that had been rumbling away at the back of Robinson's mind, leaped into his consciousness.

Rum rum yummy yum rummy rummy yummy yummy . . .

He put down the book and hunted about until he found the witch's book of spells. Turning to the last page, he read the ingredients for the making of that potion: rum and the juice of the *yummy fruit* . . .

That was all. Just two. Both of which were readily available.

What was the spell for?

He looked at the top of the page, squinting to decipher the words beneath a large brown stain. After a few seconds he exclaimed:

'Goodness me, how *extraordinary!*'

Chapter Thirty-Four
The Letter

J ack's hands began to tremble. His throat went dry. He
lifted his head and looked up and down the beach. The
sun shone; the waves tumbled against the sand; he could
feel the wind against his face. He was wide awake and sure
he was not dreaming.

And yet he must be. The message was addressed to *him*.
He unrolled the paper and began to read.

Dear Jack Bobbin,
Greetings! I hope this letter finds you
well. At least, as well as can be expected
considering your situation - and I do hope
it has not been too long delayed in the
ocean.

You may not, of course, be Jack Bobbin (very likely you are not), in which case, please replace this letter in its bottle and return it to the waves. Thank you!

If you are he, let me say first how much I have enjoyed your messages. Forgive me, that sounds rather callous and is not quite what I meant. I have been touched by your correspondence and sorely distressed by your predicament. If it were at all possible, I would certainly help you in any way that I could. I fear, however, that I can be of little use as I have no idea where in the world you are - the Atlantic is a very large ocean - and I suspect that 'searching all the local islands', as you suggest, would be pointless. I am in Cornwall, England, and I have a feeling that you are somewhere far away in the tropics.

I did make a note of the description you give of your island and, while visiting Falmouth recently, asked around among the quayside inns, which are generally full to bursting with sailors from all over the globe. Unfortunately, it seems that islands such as yours are to be found off all coasts around the Atlantic, and so I left none the wiser

163

as to your exact location. I did, however, entreat all those I met to keep a special eye out next time they passed such an island. With luck, something may come of this - I'll keep my fingers crossed! But I fear there is little else I can do.

When I said I had enjoyed your correspondence, what I really meant was that I had enjoyed the story of Robinson Crusoe. What a marvellous tale! From the moment I fished the first of your bottles out of the ocean, uncorked it and read that first page, I have been enthralled!

It was thrilling the next morning to discover another bottle, and inside it the second page of the story! And the day after that, yet another bottle and a further instalment. Well, I thought, if I keep a sharp eye out, and if these bottles keep arriving, I shall be able to discover the whole history of Robinson Crusoe, delivered to me in daily instalments!

And so it has proved. For each morning, over the past few months, a bottle has washed ashore on the beach below my cottage. Indeed, sometimes more than one. For, just when the story began to get really exciting, you thoughtfully began to send a whole lot of bottles all at once. One does like to get stuck into a story once it really gets going.

I do hope you enjoyed Robinson Crusoe's adventures as much as I did, and found them useful too no doubt? I'm sure you must have done. One thing though - a little thing, but it has bothered me. What happens on page 161? I never got that page - did you forget to send it? I scoured the shoreline for days and days but never found it. Perhaps it was lost at sea. If you do still happen to have it, you couldn't just pop it over to me, could you? I have a feeling something exciting happens at that point in the story.

One other thing - as well as the two hundred and thirty-nine pages of the Robinson Crusoe story, I also have one hundred and nineteen bottles cluttering up my small cottage. (Actually, one hundred and eighteen if you exclude the one I sent this letter in.) Anyway, although I was the landlady of an inn by profession (now retired), I have always abstained from drink myself - and people are beginning to talk! So, unless you have page 161, no more

bottles please.
Good Luck!
Yours,
Miss M Rollock

P.S. I did once know a Jack who used to listen to my stories occasionally, sitting with the children of the village on the stones outside my cottage. An absurdly improbable thought has just occurred to me . . .
I've not seen that Jack for a number of years - perhaps you are he! But no, such preposterous coincidences don't happen in real life - only in stories!

Jack was bursting with conflicting emotions when he finished reading this letter – wonder, frustration, anger, longing and dismay. He wanted to shout out across the ocean:

'It *is* me! I *am* that Jack!'

But what good would that be?

Holding the letter almost felt like *touching* his home. As if he were almost there. Yet his home was still impossibly distant.

Picking up the bottle, he ran back towards the cave.

Chapter Thirty-Five
Magic

Arriving at the freshwater spring, Jack was met by a strange sight. Robinson was standing over Caliban – who appeared to be fast asleep – holding a bottle filled with bright green liquid. He looked as though he was about to empty the liquid on to the tortoise's shell.

'What are you doing?' asked Jack, perplexed, dropping his empty bottle into the sand. But Robinson silently raised a finger and put it to his lips, as if he feared Jack might wake the tortoise.

Then he began to chant.

'*Rum rum yummy yum rummy rummy yummy yummy . . .*'

And as he chanted, he tipped the bottle so that a single drop of the bright-green liquid fell on to the shell of the tortoise – plop! For more than a minute, he continued to

chant and Jack began to think he'd gone a little mad.

At last, he stopped, and said, 'Oh well, I didn't *really* think it was going to work!'

'What? asked Jack.

Caliban opened an eye.

'Just a bit of magic,' said Robinson, pushing the cork back into the bottle.

'Magic?'

'Indeed. I discovered I had all the ingredients for one of those spells.'

'And what was all that *rummy-yummy* stuff about?'

'That was the spell. It sounds ridiculous, but . . .'

'Robinson!'

'What?'

'*Look!* Look at Caliban!'

The tortoise was shrinking . . .

'Good gracious!' cried Robinson. 'It *does* work!'

Caliban had raised his head now, a flicker of uncertainty in his eye. He was clearly aware that *something* was happening, but was it him, or was it the world around him? He was no longer the size of an upturned bathtub, but merely the size of an upturned basin . . . and then a bucket . . . and then a bowl . . . and still he shrank smaller and smaller. Fear and doubt were now clearly apparent upon his usually impassive countenance.

Jack and Robinson gaped in astonishment.

'What have you done to him, Robinson?' cried Jack.

'I've shrunk him,' replied Robinson, in an awed whisper, as he stared at the diminishing reptile. 'It's a shrinking spell.'

Caliban was now the size of a teacup . . . then an eggcup . . . and finally, a thimble. He ran around in circles like an agitated beetle, clearly in a state of utter terror.

'But, Robinson! That was a horrible, mean thing to do! Why did you do that! He may be a grumpy old tortoise, but he didn't deserve *that*!'

'No . . . No, of course you're right,' mumbled Robinson, suddenly contrite. 'I . . . I shouldn't have done it, I don't know why I did. It was a terrible thing to do. I wasn't thinking.'

'You could have shrunk a rock or something, couldn't you?'

'I should have, I just saw him lying there and looking so . . . well, so *big*. And of course, I never thought for a second it would actually *work*.'

'Well, it *did* work – and now the poor thing is just a midget tortoise, the size of those tiny tortoise shells we found!'

'But hold on, Jack, don't worry – there *is* an antidote! And if the potion worked, the antidote ought to work too. I can have him restored to normal size in no time!' He bent down and picked up another bottle. 'Same ingredients, different amounts – and same rhyme also, only chanted *backwards*. Let's try it.'

He uncorked the bottle and reaching down, tipped it up just above the tiny tortoise's shell, chanting:

'*Ymmuy ymmuy ymmur ymmur . . .*'

'WAIT!' Jack cried, so loud Robinson jumped and almost tipped the whole bottleful on to Caliban.

'What? What's the matter?'

Jack didn't answer. He was staring at Caliban, transfixed by what the tiny tortoise was doing. The minute reptile was trying to climb into the empty bottle that Jack had dropped, and which now lay in the sand at his feet. Perhaps he was looking for somewhere to hide.

Jack's anger had evaporated, he now beamed up at Robinson. 'You can do it now,' he said, 'We need to see if it works, but I've just had the most brilliant idea!'

'Oh? What's that?' asked Robinson.

'Make poor old Caliban big again, then I'll tell you.'

The antidote did work. In less than a minute Caliban was restored to his former glory and disappeared into the thorn bushes quicker than either Jack or Robinson had ever seen him move before.

'I'm a magician, Jack!' cried Robinson. 'Imagine that! I *am* Prospero!'

Jack wasn't listening. He'd picked up the empty bottle and was sitting on a rock, gazing at it, lost in thought.

'So, what's this idea of yours then? asked Robinson.

Jack held up the bottle.

'*This!*' he declared. 'This is going to be my *raft!*'

Chapter Thirty-Six
A Crazy Idea

Robinson frowned.

'What on earth do you mean, Jack?'

'I mean just what I said,' cried Jack excitedly. 'This bottle is going to be my raft! And that's how I'm going to get back home – I'm going to sail across the ocean in this bottle!'

Robinson looked aghast.

'Are you mad, Jack? That's completely bonkers!'

'No, I'm not mad. It's a brilliant idea!'

'It's a crazy idea!'

'It's not, Robinson. You just need to shrink me down small with your magic potion and put *me* into a bottle instead of a message and send *me* across the ocean!'

Robinson was incredulous. 'Jack, I know you're desperate to get home to England, but be sensible . . .'

'I *am* being sensible! I'll take some food and some water and some of that antidote potion so I can make myself big again, it'll be fine. Don't you see what a brilliant idea it is?'

Robinson was appalled.

'No, Jack, I don't see what a brilliant idea it is. You couldn't survive in a *bottle*! You'd die of thirst, or starve, or drown. And if you didn't die of those things, who knows where you'd end up?'

'I do,' replied Jack.

'What?'

'I know *exactly* where I'd end up.'

'Don't be ridiculous, Jack. You'd be drifting at the whim of the ocean currents . . .'

'And I know *exactly* where those currents would take me because I know exactly where all the other bottles have ended up.'

'What?'

'I got a reply to my messages.'

Jack handed the letter from Old Ma Rollock to Robinson.

'That letter was in this bottle. I found it in the sea this morning.'

Robinson took the sheet of paper and began to read. As he read, his frown deepened and when he'd finished, he read the whole thing again. When he looked up from the letter, he said, 'Are you saying that this letter is from the Old Ma Rollock you've told me of?'

'Yes, Robinson!' cried Jack, nodding vigorously. 'And

she lives just a few miles from my home! That little cove is where all my messages have washed ashore – I'm bound to come ashore there too!'

Robinson was silent. He looked at the letter again, shaking his head, almost unwilling to believe it was real. But it must be real.

'No, Jack,' he said at last. 'I still think it's a mad idea. I mean, *shrinking* yourself! Who knows what that will do to you?'

'Didn't hurt Caliban,' replied Jack. 'He got a shock, yes, but he was fine once he was big again.'

Robinson was still shaking his head. 'But even if the shrinking was fine, you're putting a lot of trust in what Old Ma Rollock says. Did she *really* pick up all your bottles? I mean, it's incredibly far-fetched that all your messages should end up in the same place, don't you think?'

'Why would she lie?'

'I don't know, it just seems very improbable – *more* than very improbable: impossible!'

'All the stories you tell me are extremely improbable, Robinson, and you say *they're* all true!'

Robinson shook his head, but Jack was right.

'But what about *this* letter?' Robinson argued. 'How could *her* bottle float all the way back across the ocean? That's not possible.'

'Why?'

'Because that's not the way ocean currents work,

Jack,' said Robinson, exasperated. 'They can't flow in one direction then suddenly turn around and flow in the *opposite* direction when you want them to!'

'What about a current that flows around the *edge* of the ocean, in a great big circle,' replied Jack. 'Perhaps this island is at one point in that great circle, and that cove is at another?'

Robinson could not dispute the logic of this.

'Anyway,' added Jack. 'It can't be impossible because it's happened before.'

'What do you mean?'

'Something else has sailed across the ocean from that little cove and come ashore on this island.'

'What?'

'My boat – *The Lucky Pebble*.'

'Really?' said Robinson. 'Is that where you lost it?'

Jack nodded.

'Goodness, that does seem an incredible coincidence.'

He seemed to be almost coming round to Jack's idea, but then he shook his head.

'No, the whole thing is preposterous!'

Jack merely said, 'Is it any more preposterous than magic?'

Robinson shook his head and sighed.

'I suppose you're right, but even if it is all true – and possible – even if all your bottles *did* end up in that cove . . . actually they didn't, did they? What about page one hundred and sixty-one? What happened to *that* bottle?'

'One hundred and nineteen got there, Robinson! If the chances of success are one hundred and nineteen to one, I'll take that chance!'

'But it's still a mad idea, Jack. It's not just a question of getting there – you want to survive the journey, don't you? A message doesn't have to eat or drink or breathe. You do.'

'But I can take food – I can take a whole load of yuckies – and I can take lots of bottles filled with water. I'd be tiny so I wouldn't need much.'

'Do you know they are actually called yummies?' said Robinson, changing the subject completely.

'What?'

'Yuckies – they are actually *yummies*, and they are one of the most delicious fruits in the whole world, apparently.'

'What?'

'Never mind. Anyway, what about breathing? The air inside the bottle wouldn't last forever, even if you were tiny. And you'd need to keep the cork in place otherwise it would fill up with water and sink.'

'I could . . . I could make a very small air hole in the cork. It would let in air but hardly any water, I'm sure that could work!'

But Robinson was still shaking his head.

Then Jack said, 'You seem to be so dead against the idea, anyone would think you didn't *want* me to get back home. I thought this whole message in a bottle thing was a way of helping me escape from this island. It was your plan,

Robinson. And you had such faith in it. Well, you were right – it's worked! Sort of. But now you don't want me to escape.'

Robinson changed his tone.

'Of course, I do, Jack! Of course, I do! It's just all so improbable, and for your plan to succeed, you'd still need an awful lot of *luck* . . .'

'But that's just it, Robinson – that's exactly why I believe in it! You said once you thought I was the luckiest boy in the world. Well – maybe I am! I think it's all *meant* to happen – all the bottles ending up in that cove in Cornwall; finding the spell book and that shrinking spell – it *is* all amazingly lucky! And you believe in luck, don't you?' He paused and thrust his hand into his trouser pocket and extracted his little black pebble.

'Besides, I have a lucky pebble! So, everything's bound to be all right in the end!'

Robinson was silent. He had nothing else to say. Jack seemed to have an answer to all his arguments. And perhaps Jack was right.

'Look,' he said at last, 'let's sleep on it, shall we? You have a proper think about it, and I will too, and then, if you're still dead set on the idea tomorrow morning, well . . . well, of course I'll try and help you make it work, Jack.'

'Really?'

'Yes, really.'

Jack walked over, put his arms around Robinson's waist

and gave him a hug.

'Thank you, Robinson,' he said, pressing his cheek against Robinson's tummy.

'That's all right, Jack,' mumbled Robinson, gently patting Jack's head. 'That's quite all right.'

Chapter Thirty-Seven
Caliban Gets A New Name

Jack spent the rest of the morning sitting on the rocks above the pool, tying fiddly knots in lengths of cotton and cutting corks in half and poking holes through them. Robinson experimented with his magic potion; Jack could hear his chanting coming from the sandy courtyard. Around midday, however, the chanting suddenly stopped, and Robinson emerged from the alley between the boulders carrying a large earthenware bowl. He marched purposefully away, heading north.

'Robinson? Where are you going?' called Jack.

Robinson called back over his shoulder:

'I must find Caliban!'

Caliban? thought Jack. *Is there something* else *scratched on his shell?* He ran after Robinson.

'Why?' he asked, catching up. 'And what's the bowl for?'

'I see it all now,' declared Robinson, ignoring Jack's question. 'The history of that unfortunate beast – I understand it, and I see what a truly terrible thing I have done!' He seemed quite distressed. '*Caliban!* Why did I ever give him *that* name? Caliban was the offspring of Sycorax! He shall never be called that again, the noble beast! Odysseus or Hercules would be more appropriate – he is both clever and strong!'

Caliban probably *wasn't* an appropriate name now they knew about the witch, but Jack couldn't see why this was making Robinson so distressed.

Moments later Robinson got down on his hands and knees and crawled under a bush. Jack assumed he'd found Caliban until, peering under the bush, he saw that Robinson was picking up fallen yuckies and putting them into the earthenware bowl. Rotten yuckies. The rottenest yuckies he could find. Soft, gooey, decomposing fruits that oozed and dripped and collapsed into a sludgy mess as he picked them up.

'What are you *doing*, Robinson? That's horrible!' cried Jack. 'Don't touch those!'

Robinson ignored him and continued to drop the fruits into the bowl. When it was full, he crawled out from under the bush and began to lick his slimy fingers.

'*Robinson!* Yuck!' cried Jack, appalled. 'You'll be sick!'

But far from being sick, Robinson's eyes widened with

evident delight, and he began to lick more vigorously. Grinning broadly, he said:

'My, that *is* good! That's *remarkably* good! That's the most delicious thing I have ever tasted in my whole life! Here, try some, Jack.'

He thrust the bowl of blackened rotten fruit towards Jack. But Jack retreated, his mouth twisted in disgust.

'No, you're right, I should save these,' said Robinson, shaking his head. 'They're for Cali . . . that noble tortoise, not us! But they *are* delicious, Jack. We were fools eating those horrible ripe fruits, they're meant to be eaten when they're *rotten*, like this! No wonder that noble beast looked at us as if we were idiots!'

'But *why* are you collecting fruit for Caliban?' asked Jack, 'or whatever we're meant to call him now?'

'Hercules, I think. That's what we'll call him.'

'Hercules, then, but why?'

'A peace offering,' said Robinson. 'Something to atone for my shocking actions. I've no idea what else to give him, but he'll surely enjoy a bowlful of these!'

Robinson then began to explain that he'd come to understand the history of the tortoise. 'He was once part of a great colony of noble giant tortoises,' he said, 'who had lived on this island in undisturbed seclusion for goodness knows how many millennia . . . until that witch arrived.

'She'd brought with her the book of magic spells but having none of the ingredients to make her potions, she devised a new potion using yummy fruits and rum – a shrinking potion.

'I imagine she took some malicious pleasure in what she did with it, enjoying the twisted irony perhaps. She used her potion to shrink the giant tortoises.

'From grand and prodigious reptiles, she turned them into little beetle-sized things. From masters – *monarchs* – of this island they were reduced to complete insignificance, prey to any passing seagull or even rat! Poor creatures. And what *Hercules* must have felt, as he witnessed this – as he saw his brothers and sisters, his cousins, his aunts and uncles, *shrunk* – goodness knows! All the while expecting it to be his fate too! And there seemed to be nothing he could do about it.

'And yet he *did* do something, the clever reptile.

'Giant tortoises, I have learned, seek out the shade in the middle of the day. The heat of the noonday sun would cook them in their shells if they didn't. There is one place on this whole island where that colony of giant tortoises could rest in the shade together: that deep gully where the sun's rays never penetrate. It was there that those giant tortoises gathered in the middle of the day. A thing they must have continued to do even when they'd been shrunk down small. This was noticed by the witch, and, as if shrinking them wasn't enough, she decided to collect the unfortunate little tortoises as trophies. What particular fate befell them we'll never know, but their shells ended up strung on a thread around that witch's neck.

'A day came when Hercules alone, of all his clan, retained his proper proportions. He'd witnessed the witch catching the tiny tortoises, and when he saw her approaching the gully, he crept up on to the mound that rose above it. Atop the mound, he put his shell against the great stone that stood sentinel there. And waited. The witch stepped down into the gully. She reached down to pick up a tiny tortoise shell. Hercules pushed, heaved, strained with all his might against the stone.

'It shifted . . .

'It toppled . . .

'You know the result. It was Hercules who killed the witch and saved those that remained of his tribe, though only *he* remained a truly giant tortoise.

'And what did I do to him this morning?'

'You . . . you *shrank* him, Robinson,' said Jack.

Robinson nodded, mournfully.

They eventually found Hercules at the far northern tip of the island, among the rocks where the gulls nested. Jack felt terrible when he saw real terror in eyes of the tortoise as they approached. Robinson must have felt worse. There was no way Hercules could escape them of course; instead he retracted his head and limbs into his shell.

Robinson knelt, bowing his head, and placing the bowl of rotten yummies before the beast.

'Forgive me,' he said, in a voice full of remorse. 'It was a terrible thing I did, but I never meant you any harm. I should have thought, but honestly, I never for one moment believed the magic would really work!'

He went on, speaking with such persuasive eloquence that even the stoniest of hearts would surely have melted and granted him absolution. But the tortoise remained unmoved.

Whether he understood anything of what Robinson was saying is doubtful, but he must have got a sense of it from the tone of Robinson's wonderfully expressive voice.

Yet still the tortoise remained in his shell.

'I don't think he's going to come out, Robinson,' said Jack at last.

Robinson shook his head, sadly. 'No. And why should he? I've merely confirmed his low opinion of humanity.

And who could disagree with him?'

They left the bowl and began to walk back to the cave.

'Look!' cried Jack, glancing over his shoulder after about fifty yards or so.

Robinson looked.

Hercules was greedily tucking into the bowl of rotten yummies.

Chapter Thirty-Eight
Jack's Bottle

Next morning Jack found Robinson sitting out in the courtyard, chuckling to himself.

'Look at that!' he cried, holding out a hand as Jack approached. Jack peered into his outstretched palm and saw a pile of . . . of what? Coarse sand? Some dried vegetable matter? He looked closer. It was a heap of tiny books!

'That's the Bible,' said Robinson, 'and the complete works of Shakespeare and Homer and Plato and Aesop and Dante and Chaucer and Milton and . . . well, whoever else you'd care to name! Much of the wisdom of all mankind, lying in the palm of my hand! And I can carry it all around in my pocket – a library in my pocket, imagine that! And if ever I want to read one of them, I just drop a little of my antidote potion on it and there it is! Amazing, don't you think?'

'Fantastic,' agreed Jack. 'It's a brilliant idea, Robinson. But look at this bottle I've been working on.' He lifted the bottle he was carrying.

'Still dead set on going then?'

Jack nodded.

Robinson tipped the little pile of books into a silver snuff box, closed the lid and put it into his pocket. 'Let's have a look at it then.'

Jack handed him the bottle. 'I've made a kind of rope ladder with cotton, Robinson, can you see? Not very good – it's much too fiddly making those tiny knots, but I can make it better when I'm small. Do you see how I've attached it, winding the cotton around the outside neck, then dropping the ladder down inside? That should be secure, shouldn't it?'

Robinson nodded. 'What about the cork?'

Jack pulled a cork out of his pocket. He'd cut it down to about a quarter of its normal length and tied a thread around it, at the other end of which was a stone with a hole in the middle. This rested on the bottom of the bottle.

'The cork fits snug and quite tight, but not too tight, I hope,' explained Jack. 'Of course, I'll only be able to test if I can push it out when I'm small. I should be able to; it's quite a *thin* cork now. The stone just fits through the bottle neck, and will stop me losing the cork when it's pushed out. What do you think?'

Robinson held up the bottle and carefully examined the

cork, the thread and the stone inside it.

'It *ought* to work,' he said at last. 'But we'll need to test it in the pool first with a cargo on board.'

'Can we test it *now*, Robinson?' cried Jack, eagerly. 'Then I'll start collecting yuckies – or, what were they? *Yummies!* Ha!'

Before Robinson could answer, Jack had run out of the courtyard.

They tested the seaworthiness of the bottle by filling it almost half full of sand and launching it in the pool. It floated beautifully and straight away, Jack set about collecting yummies.

That evening they stood before a great pile of provisions gathered on the sand beside the freshwater pool. As well as hundreds of yummies, there was a bundle of stiff dried fish and numerous bottles of spring water.

'I can't believe all *that* is going to fit into *this* bottle!' said Jack, looking at the bottle in his hand.

'I'm sure it will, Jack – once it's small. But even all this, I fear, will not be enough.'

'But there's loads and loads here!'

'I know – but you'll be at sea for months and months, a whole year perhaps. I think you ought to take this, then you can catch some fish.' He picked up his fishing spear, which was lying in the sand at his feet.

'But you'll need that!' protested Jack.

'Nonsense, I can easily make another one. You'll only be catching tiddlers, of course, but a tiddler could feed you for a whole week.'

He laid the fishing spear down beside the other things, then picked up a wooden pail.

'You'll need this too,' he said.

'Er, is that for what I think it's for?' asked Jack, a little dubiously.

'Oh, no – I thought you could sit on the bottle rim to do *that*! This is for collecting seawater.'

'Why do I need seawater? I can't drink it.'

'Not for drinking, for ballast, Jack. All those yummies will, with any luck, keep the bottle floating buoyantly upright – like the keel of a boat that extends down below the hull – but as you eat them, the bottle will gradually lose stability and tip sideways. You'll need to replace their weight with seawater. You can tie this pail to a line to collect it. I'm afraid you are eventually going to have a pool of seawater at the bottom of your bottle, but it can't be helped. I'll find some small straight sticks that you can use to make an internal structure within the bottle, so you don't end up *sitting* in the pool by the end of your voyage.'

'You're so clever, Robinson. You think of everything!'

'I don't! I'm sure there's a major flaw in your plan that we *haven't* thought of yet. But anyway, here's another thing I *have* thought of.'

He picked up what seemed to be a circular piece of sail-cloth with some straightish wooden struts sewn on to it, all radiating from a small hole at its centre.

'I made this while you were picking yummies,' he said.

'Er . . . what is it?' asked Jack.

'It's a *rain catcher*, of course! At least, I hope it is. It's not been tested, but it ought to work. When it rains you push out the cork and open it out like a funnel above the top of the bottle – the bottle you're in, that is – while holding the bottle you want to fill just below the hole. One drop of rain should just about fill a bottle.'

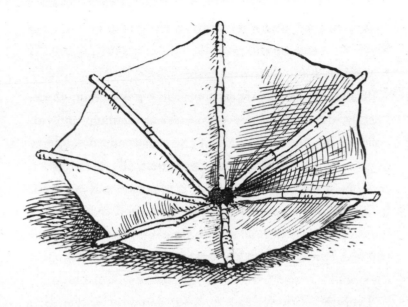

'You *do* think of everything!'

Robinson shook his head and replied, 'I'm sure I haven't.'

'You *have*, Robinson,' Jack insisted. 'I just know it's going to work! Shall we start the shrinking?'

Before they started, however, Robinson said, 'You do know, Jack, that you won't be able to take all that gold? It'll be far too heavy, even when shrunk.'

'Of course, Robinson. I don't want it. I just want to get home.'

'You should be able to take a little of it though.'

'No, it's fine, Robinson. I won't take any.'

'Well, I've filled a little pouch here. I think you should take that – just enough for a new thatch and a farm cart and such like.'

Jack nodded, and Robinson laid the pouch on the sand beside the other provisions.

And then the shrinking began.

It didn't take nearly as long as it might have done. Luckily, they didn't have to shrink every yummy individually, which could have taken them days and days. They discovered that things of a similar nature, all piled together, could be shrunk with just one drop of potion and one spell. In less than an hour everything had been reduced to a hundredth of its normal size and put into the bottle. And still the bottle bobbed buoyantly upright when floated in the pool.

Everything was ready.

'My turn now,' said Jack, excitedly.

'Your turn?'

'To be shrunk!'

'What – *now?*'

'Why not?'

Robinson shrugged. 'Oh . . . I thought . . . Shouldn't you wait a little, Jack? Just a few days – to be absolutely sure you want to do this?'

'I *am* sure! I can't wait a few days! But I'll wait until tomorrow, Robinson. I'll go tomorrow morning.'

Robinson could see that all Jack was thinking about now was getting back to his home. 'All right,' he said, 'tomorrow it is then.'

That evening, sitting before a fire on the beach, they both felt strangely awkward. The easy companionship of other evenings was somehow missing, and their conversation felt forced. In the end, they sat in silence, and then Robinson shuffled up beside Jack and put an arm around his shoulders, and the silence didn't matter. When the moon rose, they kicked sand on to the fire and went to bed.

Late in the night Jack was still wide awake.

'Robinson?' he said, for he could sense that Robinson was wide awake also.

'Yes, Jack?'

'Why don't you come with me?'

There was silence for a long minute before Robinson said, 'This is my home, Jack. I'm perfectly happy here.'

'I just thought . . .' began Jack, but then fell silent.

'Don't you worry about me, Jack, I'll be fine!' said Robinson. 'Besides, there's not really room for two in that bottle – not enough provisions. And a big fellow like me would certainly sink it!'

Chapter Thirty-Nine
The Lucky Bottle

'Your bottle should have a name, Jack,' said Robinson, as they stood on the beach the next morning. 'All boats have names. May I suggest *The Lucky Bottle*? It'll certainly *need* to be a lucky bottle!'

Jack thought that was the perfect name.

As well as Jack's 'boat' there were three other bottles standing on the sand at their feet. Two small ones of red and green glass, and a full bottle of rum.

'The naming of boats is usually done by smashing a bottle of wine over the bow,' said Robinson, 'but we haven't any wine and that would be a highly dangerous thing to do to *this* boat! I suggest we splash a little rum over her?'

So, Robinson uncorked the bottle of rum and splashed a little over Jack's bottle, saying:

'I name this vessel *The Lucky Bottle*! May she bring luck to all who sail in her! Well, to Jack Bobbin, at least!'

Jack applauded loudly.

'And now you need to put *these* in your pockets,' said Robinson, putting aside the rum and picking up the coloured bottles. One contained the shrinking potion and the other, the antidote.

'You won't need much – just a drop. And though I don't suppose you'll need the *shrinking* potion once you're small, you'd better have some, just in case. Remember: red for shrinking, green for getting big again – got that?'

Jack nodded.

'I'd keep them in separate pockets if I were you – so they don't smash against each other. Red in the right pocket, green in the left.'

Jack put the bottles into his pockets. Robinson then handed him a small piece of paper, saying: 'Here are the spells to go with each potion. I'd memorize them too, just in case you lose that. They're easy to learn; very repetitious! Now, are you ready?'

Jack nodded.

'Check your pockets again. Where did you put that paper?'

Jack thrust his hands into his pockets and pulled out the bottles and the folded piece of paper. He showed them to Robinson.

Robinson nodded. 'Now, here are a few other things I

thought of last night, as well at those sticks I mentioned – for the internal structure.'

He took a bundled-up handkerchief from his pocket and unfolded it. Inside were half a dozen lengths of stick, seven or eight inches long but less than the thickness of a pencil. 'You can use part of the handkerchief to make a hammock, and the rest for blankets, maybe – it's liable to be quite cold at night, and it certainly will be when you get into more northerly waters. There's also some extra cotton – you're bound to need that – and somewhere in that handkerchief is your boat, *The Lucky Pebble*. I've already shrunk it. Oh, and a little bottle of rum too, just in case you lose one of the potions. I've put the recipe on that paper with the spells, so you'll be able to make some more. And . . . where is it? There! Do you see that?'

Jack looked to where Robinson was pointing and saw something very small glinting in the sun.

'A knife!' said Robinson. 'Absolutely essential!'

Of course it was. Why hadn't Jack thought of it himself? What would he have done without a knife?

Robinson dropped the things from the handkerchief into *The Lucky Bottle*, then stuffed in the handkerchief itself, before putting the bottle down on the sand at his feet.

Everything was ready.

'You're sure about this?' said Robinson.

'Yes, Robinson.'

Robinson nodded. 'Jack,' he said, holding out a hand, 'it's

been an absolute pleasure to know you! I've had the most wonderful time these last two years, the best time of my life! And though I said I'd get along fine without you, I shall miss you desperately – for a while at least.'

They shook hands, and Jack, unable to speak for fear he would cry, stepped forward and hugged Robinson tightly.

'Thank you!' was all he could manage.

Robinson wiped away a tear himself, then said, 'Right – are you *sure* you're ready?'

'Yes,' said Jack.

Robinson took a bottle of the shrinking potion from his pocket and was about to pull out the cork when Jack said:

'Look!'

He pointed to the top of the beach. Hercules had emerged from the bushes and was looking down to where they stood near the breaking waves. Jack waved to him.

'Goodbye, Hercules!' he called. 'I'm sorry we never quite got to be friends, but I really appreciate all your help with the treasure hunt – we would certainly never have found it without you!'

Hercules nodded, raising and dropping his head, up and down.

'He's nodding!' cried Jack. 'He's not shaking his head from side to side, like he always does, he's nodding! I think he's saying goodbye and wishing me luck, Robinson!'

'Yes, it certainly looks that way!' said Robinson in wonder. Then he pulled the cork from the bottle of potion and lifted it up above Jack's head.

'Here goes then,' he said, and as he slowly tipped the bottle, he began to chant: '*Rum rum yummy yum rummy rummy yummy yummy . . .*'

Nothing happened for a moment, then suddenly Jack felt a tingling sensation all over his body, and he noticed that Robinson was growing bigger . . .

And bigger . . .

And BIGGER . . .

Rising higher and higher into the sky, so that Jack was forced to crane his neck further and further back to keep his eyes fixed on Robinson's fast ascending face, until at last, Robinson towered high above him, a monumental giant.

Just in front of Jack, Robinson's big toe rested on the sand like an enormous boulder.

What Hercules must have thought as he watched Jack being shrunk is impossible to know. Perhaps he understood about Jack's crazy plan? Perhaps he understood a lot more than they'd ever given him credit for.

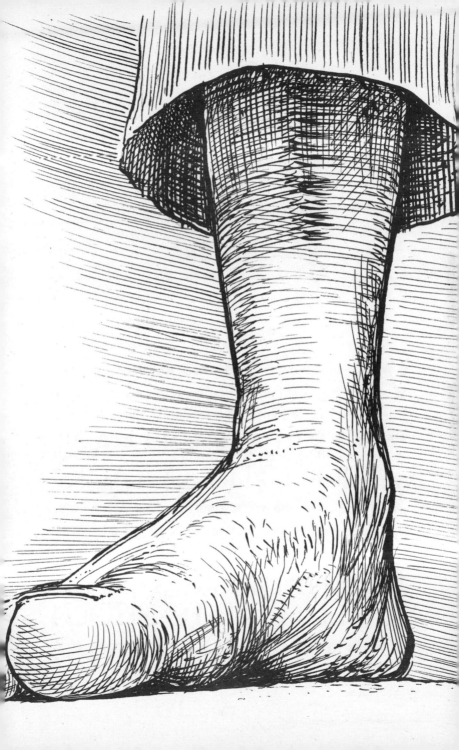

Chapter Forty
Shrunk!

'**A**re you all right, Jack?' asked Robinson, anxiously peering down at the tiny figure on the sand just in front of his foot. What Jack heard sounded more like this:

'AAARRE YOOOU AAALLL RRIIIIGGHHTT JAAACK?'

A great booming voice, rumbling like distant thunder. When Jack replied: 'Yes, I think so,' he sounded like a tiny squeak, which Robinson could barely hear.

'SORRY, JACK? I THINK YOU'LL HAVE TO SHOUT.'

Robinson knelt down, bending over and cupping an ear towards Jack.

'ALL RIGHT, ROBINSON,' shouted Jack. 'BUT IF I SHOUT, CAN YOU WHISPER – YOU'RE RATHER DEAFENING!'

'Yes of course – how's this?'

'BETTER.'

They both stared at each other.

'You look . . . *different*, Jack,' said Robinson.

'SO DO YOU! RATHER TERRIFYING! AND THAT GREAT BEARD OF YOURS – I COULD GET LOST IN THERE AND NEVER FIND MY WAY OUT!'

Robinson raised his head a little, stroking his beard. It sounded to Jack like a high wind, rustling through a forest of pine trees.

Your voice sounds much higher, Jack,' said Robinson. 'Squeakier, *quicker*. And you move quicker too – like a jerky little insect.'

'*YOU* SOUND MUCH SLOWER, ROBINSON, AND DEEPER. AND YOU SEEM TO BE MOVING IN SLOW MOTION.'

Robinson lowered his right hand and rested it, palm up, on the sand beside Jack.

'Can you climb on to my hand?' he said.

Jack scrambled up on to Robinson's index finger, then walked along it and into the middle of his palm where he sat down. Then Robinson lifted Jack until he was level with his enormous face.

Speaking much more quietly, he said, 'Let's see how

you get on inside the bottle, shall we?' And reaching
down with his left hand he picked up *The Lucky Bottle* and
held his right-hand flush with the top of it. Jack stepped
into the bottle and climbed down the cotton thread rope
ladder.

When he was standing on the pile of yummies, Robinson
said, 'Watch out, Jack – here comes the stone.'

And he lowered the stone, dangling from the cork, into
the bottle. It got stuck in the opening briefly and he jiggled
it a little to get it to slip in. Jack stood clear, against the side
of the bottle, as the stone descended and came to rest on
the yummies. The cork at the other end of the thread was
still outside the bottle, hanging just below the top.

'Get hold of the cotton, Jack,' instructed Robinson. 'See if you can pull the cork into place.'

Jack took hold of the cotton rope with both hands and pulled. The cork rose up, turned over and slipped into place perfectly.

'Excellent, Jack! Now run up the ladder and see if you can push it out.'

Jack climbed the ladder, braced his feet against the sides of the bottle's neck, put his shoulder to the cork and pushed. Out it popped.

'Marvellous! That seems to work perfectly!'

'I KNEW IT WOULD!' cried Jack, standing on the top rung of the ladder.

Robinson looked out across the ocean. There was barely a breeze, and the waves were calm and gentle. Perfect weather to begin a voyage.

'You're absolutely sure about this, Jack?' he asked.

'I AM,' replied Jack.

'All right, here goes!'

And Robinson waded out into the water until the waves were sloshing up around his middle, then lifting the bottle to his face, he said:

'Well . . . Goodbye, Jack Bobbin.'

'GOODBYE, ROBINSON,' replied Jack. Then he climbed down the rope ladder, pulled the cork into place above him . . . and Robinson set *The Lucky Bottle* adrift in the ocean.

Chapter Forty-One
A Terrible Mistake

For several minutes, Robinson watched as the bottle drifted away, bobbing among the waves. Then, unable to bear the sight any longer, he turned and waded back to the shore. He saw that Hercules had come down on to the beach to where he and Jack had been standing moments before. He was still nodding . . . no, he wasn't nodding, he was reaching down to the sand and touching something with his nose, then raising his head and looking at Robinson. Robinson looked down at what he'd touched . . . then, with a gasp of horror, he reached down and picked it up.

'What have I done?' he cried, turning, and running back down to the sea and splashing out into the waves.

'What *terrible*, foolish thing have I done?'

Tears were streaming down his cheeks as he crashed through the breakers, deeper and deeper, the salty ocean slapping against his face.

But it was too late.

The bottle was gone.

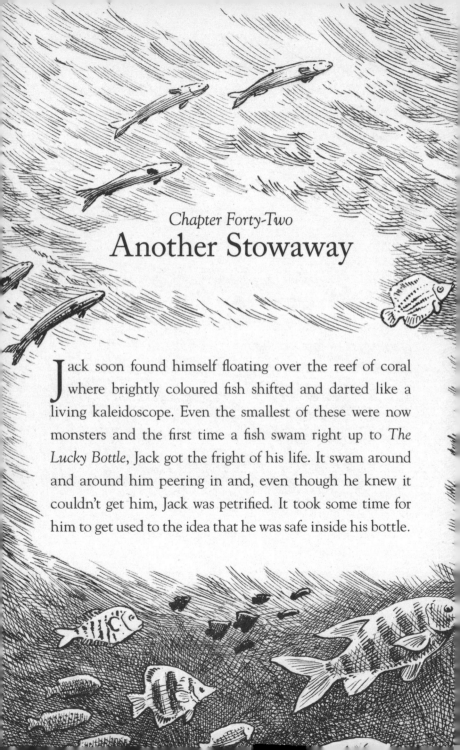

Chapter Forty-Two
Another Stowaway

Jack soon found himself floating over the reef of coral where brightly coloured fish shifted and darted like a living kaleidoscope. Even the smallest of these were now monsters and the first time a fish swam right up to *The Lucky Bottle*, Jack got the fright of his life. It swam around and around him peering in and, even though he knew it couldn't get him, Jack was petrified. It took some time for him to get used to the idea that he was safe inside his bottle.

By afternoon, he'd passed over the reef and was drifting above flat, featureless sand, stretching away in the dim distance. He saw great rays swimming by in graceful, slow-motion flight, like huge carpets with tails, and down on the seabed flat fish zoomed along sending up cloudy trails, like horses galloping along dusty roads. There were giant spider crabs too, with long, spindly, stilt-like legs, wandering ponderously across the sand. Gradually, however, the floor of the ocean dropped away below the bottle, and then disappeared altogether, and Jack was floating above fathoms and fathoms of dark water.

He never saw the seabed again for the rest of his voyage.

Just as the light was fading, he became aware of a sound. A kind of low hum, almost a vibration. He looked out into the water around the bottle but could see nothing. Could fish make noises? He knew that dolphins and whales could. Robinson had once told him that whales sang songs that travelled for miles and miles through the ocean. Perhaps a whale was singing somewhere far away.

The sound gradually became louder and until it actually *was* a vibration; travelling up his legs from the yummies he was standing on.

The sound, he realized, it was coming from *inside* the bottle.

It sharpened and became a distinct *buzz* . . . and suddenly the yummies below Jack's feet began to move. He jumped back, grabbing the rope ladder just as a long, segmented leg, covered in black spiky hairs, emerged from the pile of fruits. A second leg thrust upwards followed by a great head with giant bulbous eyes. Jack was on the rope ladder now, climbing as fast as he could and looking down between his feet as the thing heaved itself out from beneath the yummies, like a corpse emerging from a grave.

It was a gigantic fly.

Free of the yummies, it took off and began to zigzag back and forth across the bottle, bashing itself against the glass. The buzzing was almost deafening.

Jack, at the top of the rope ladder, put his shoulder against the cork and pushed. But the cork wouldn't budge. The buzzing suddenly stopped. He looked down and to his horror, saw that the fly was crawling up the ladder towards him. He pushed harder; he pushed with all his might. But still the cork wouldn't budge. He was finding it difficult to brace his feet against the sides of the bottle neck. They were slipping; he was drenched in sweat. His heart was pounding, he was trembling, his breathing was short and shallow. He felt too weak to push out the cork.

Then the fly's hairy leg touched his foot and he kicked out, almost losing his hold on the rope ladder. It was there, just below him. He could see every detail of its huge dull-red eyes . . . its twitching mouthparts.

He bent his knees and back, took a deep breath, pushed his slipping feet hard against the bottle and sprang up, hitting the cork above with all the strength he could muster.

It popped out.

He gripped the bottle rim, pulled himself up, out and down over the side, hanging on to the thread, dangling with the cork against the outside of the bottle. The fly crawled out, paused briefly, then buzzed away into the twilight.

Chapter Forty-Three
The First Night

B ack inside the bottle, Jack wondered how the fly had got in. It must have been among the pile of yummies when Robinson had shrunk them. And because only things of a similar nature were affected by the shrinking spell, the fly had remained its normal size. They should have checked the tiny yummies before they put them in the bottle. Now he couldn't help thinking there might be other flies among the fruits piled up below him, and as the light faded he felt more than a little apprehensive about the night ahead.

He slept uneasily when he did sleep. And lying in the pitch-black darkness, he wished he had a light. Why had he forgotten to bring a lantern? Why hadn't Robinson thought of that? He'd thought of everything else.

But then again, perhaps a lantern wouldn't have been

such a good idea after all. A light shining in the endless darkness of the night-time ocean might attract unwanted attention. Who knew what creatures it might draw up from the depths?

That thought made him even more uneasy, and for the rest of the night he couldn't stop thinking about what might be lurking in the black waters below him.

It was then, on that first night, that Jack began to fully understand the enormity of what he had embarked upon. And he wished with all his heart that he was back on the island sitting by a fire on the beach with Robinson.

It was a long night. A *very* long night – and not just because he slept badly. It seemed to go on for ever and ever; far longer than any night Jack had ever experienced before. And when at last, the first rays of the rising sun caught the neck of *The Lucky Bottle*, Jack almost cried out for joy. He ran up the rope ladder, pushing out the cork to look upon the new day, and more than half wishing that the bottle had somehow drifted back to the island, and that he'd see the familiar outline of the rocky outcrop rising in the morning mist.

But he saw only ocean and sky. And the swell was broad and deep. He knew he must be far from any land.

After a breakfast of two yummies, he set about building a structure within the bottle, as Robinson had suggested. Using the knife, he cut various lengths of stick. Some shorter pieces he wedged crossways across the bottle, while

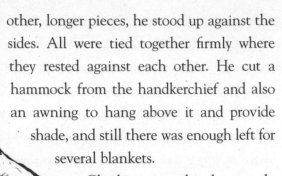

other, longer pieces, he stood up against the sides. All were tied together firmly where they rested against each other. He cut a hammock from the handkerchief and also an awning to hang above it and provide shade, and still there was enough left for several blankets.

Climbing into his hammock, Jack was pleased to find it was very comfortable, partly because it was not lumpy and bumpy like the bed of yummies, but mostly because it was *still*. He realized how much tension had built up in all his muscles, which were continually having to compensate for the motion of the bottle tipping this way and that with the rise and fall of the waves. The movement of the hammock was not governed by the ocean but by the steady constant of gravity. He began to feel properly relaxed and almost cheerful, and the aching regret and desperation of the night before began to fade.

Maybe things were going to be all right after all.

As he lay there, he noticed something moving out in the ocean. Fish – lots and lots of them; little fish – though not so little for Jack. They began to gather around the bottle, a great shimmering cloud, swimming around and around, peering in at him. And then, in an instant, they were gone, and Jack was left wondering if he'd somehow frightened them. Then he looked down into the waters below the bottle and saw blue tiger-striped shapes zooming by. Mackerel.

With a flash of bright turquoise, one turned and swam up towards the bottle. Others followed and in seconds there were hundreds of them swarming around *The Lucky Bottle*; pushing, jostling, bumping, snapping at the glass, working themselves into a frenzy, trying to get at Jack. The bottle was bashed and buffeted this way and that, and Jack, who'd climbed out of his hammock, lost his footing, and was tossed about with the yummies and all the other bits and pieces stowed in the bottle. He worried that the bottles of fresh water might be smashed. But then as suddenly as they'd appeared, the mackerel too were gone, leaving just a scale or two falling through the water like silvery autumn leaves.

Jack looked down again and saw, rising from the depths, the grey shape of an enormous shark.

Chapter Forty-Four
The Shark

Up and up it rose until it was just below *The Lucky Bottle*. And for Jack, it was ten times bigger than the biggest whale he could ever imagine. It rolled to one side, tilting its vast head, so that its great black eye could look up into the bottle. And it seemed to be looking directly at Jack. Slowly, it glided past just inches away on the other side of the glass; its colossal grinning mouth; its jagged rows of

tombstone-sized teeth . . . and there came into Jack's mind something Robinson had said:

'Sharks will eat almost anything – that one I caught with a mop had just eaten a bucket!'

Jack wondered if the shark might swallow his bottle.

And then he remembered something else. He remembered the bottle that Old Ma Rollock had never received. The bottle containing page 161. Had that been swallowed by a shark?

He hardly dared to breathe as the great fish's body passed the bottle, on and on and on, until finally with a flick of its gigantic tail it set the bottle spinning and was gone. Jack didn't move for another half hour, fearing the shark's return.

It didn't. Not that day. But would there be other sharks? Jack began to realize how horribly vulnerable his little bottle was, drifting aimlessly in the great ocean.

He thought of all the other creatures besides sharks that might be swimming in the waters below the bottle. And now that he was tiny, almost everything down there was a monster.

Chapter Forty-Five
The Fatal Flaw

He saw no sharks the next day, nor any other fish. A week passed, a long, slow week of interminable days and endless lonely nights, and it felt more like a *month* to Jack. In all that time he saw nothing in the waters around his bottle. His fear and trepidation gradually faded, to be replaced by mind-numbing boredom. And with nothing to do but lie in his hammock looking out into the empty ocean, he found his thoughts constantly fixed upon the one thing that relieved the monotony of those wearisome hours: food.

Robinson had filled several jars with delicious rotten yummies. 'These can be a special treat,' he'd said. 'I suggest just a spoonful a day. And by the time you've finished them all the others will have begun to rot.'

But Jack ate more than just one spoonful a day. He ate a lot more. He couldn't help himself. He craved the rotten yummies and could think of little else. Within two weeks all the jars were empty. And so were the four jars of shellfish pickled in rum. And Jack had munched his way through all the stiff dried fish also. After three weeks, only the ripe green yummies remained. And Jack began to eat those as greedily as he had the rotten fruit in the jars. Which was strange. He chastised himself continually for his unforgivable greed, and yet he couldn't help it. And it wasn't just the tedious emptiness of his days at sea that drove his desire to eat all the time. He really was ravenously *hungry*.

And he was always thirsty too. The bottles of water were emptying worryingly fast and not a drop of rain had fallen in all the weeks he'd been at sea. Robinson's ingenious rain catcher lay folded and redundant. But even so, he was quite unable to ration himself to just a few mouthfuls of water each day.

What was the matter with him? Why was he so hungry and so thirsty? He was mortified by his weakness of will. At this rate, his supplies would run out long before *The Lucky Bottle* ever reached England. And yet still, he couldn't help himself.

It took him some time to fully understand his predicament, and this, he only realized after he'd remembered *caterpillars* . . .

He'd once watched a caterpillar eating its way around

the edges of a leaf. A leaf that was far larger than the caterpillar itself, and yet the creature chomped and chomped away until all that remained was a scraggy bit of stalk. And then it had crawled along to the next leaf and began to eat that. Jack had wondered how the caterpillar managed to eat so much. He could never have eaten as much, even if he was eating jam and scones and pasties, his favourite foods. He would have burst.

How was it that the caterpillar didn't?

He understood now. He understood that it was all to do with *time*.

He had thought that time was the same for everybody and everything. But he now realized that it wasn't. Time is relative. It's different for caterpillars. As it is for all small creatures. A day for a caterpillar is an awful lot longer than a day is for a human being. And though Jack had always thought that small things lived *shorter* lives – the smaller the creature the shorter the life – this wasn't true. They lived *quicker* lives. Time for them, was passing much *faster*.

And this, of course, explained why there had been no tiny tortoises left on the island. Their lives had been just as long as Hercules' would be. They'd just lived their lives *quicker*.

Jack was a small creature now and so a single day really was, for him, more like a week. No wonder he was always

hungry. He'd need more than just three meals a day. He wasn't being greedy at all. And no wonder he found it impossible to ration himself to just a few mouthfuls of water a day. He'd die of thirst if he didn't drink more.

This was the major flaw in the plan that Robinson had been sure was there. The flaw that neither he nor Jack had seen. The strange paradox that the smaller Jack was, the more he'd need to eat and drink. Not because he'd be hungrier, but because, in effect, he'd be at sea for far, far longer.

Six months was the time they had judged it would take *The Lucky Bottle* to reach England, but for tiny Jack it would really be years and years.

If he ever got there at all.

And unless he managed to catch some fish – and some rain – that was looking extremely unlikely.

Standing at the top of the rope ladder, Jack would lean out of the bottle clutching the fishing spear and waiting for hour upon hour. But the seas remained empty of fish. He'd scan the horizon for clouds and the chance of rain, ready to run down and grab the rain catcher. But the skies remained endlessly blue.

Day by day, the bottles of fresh water were gradually drained and the pile of yummies reduced, until soon there was just a few bottles of water left and a small heap of yummies. These, he eventually transferred to an improvised sack he'd made from one of the handkerchief blankets, which was now hanging from one of the crosswise sticks. The remaining bottles of fresh water were in there too.

For some while now, he'd been collecting a pail or two of seawater every day to act as ballast, as Robinson had suggested. He'd push out the cork, drop the pail into the sea and then haul it up. A pool of salty water now sloshed about at the bottom of the bottle.

Paradoxically, as the yummies began to turn brown and mushy, they tasted more and more delicious, and harder and harder to resist. Trying to ration what he ate became an unbearable torture.

He thought of Robinson a lot. Especially at night as he lay clutching the sea-worn fragment of his little boat, shivering at the idea of all the infinite darkness that surrounded him. He wished with all his heart he was back on the island, sitting by a fire on the beach, listening to Robinson telling one of his outlandish stories, or reading to him, or performing one of Shakespeare's plays.

With the full realization that he'd never ever see Robinson again, a black despair came upon him.

Chapter Forty-Six
A Dream

A day came when there was just one bottle of fresh water left and only ten yummies. A change had come over Jack. No longer did he stand at the top of the rope ladder, spear in hand, or look up at the sky for any sign of rain. A great lethargy had descended upon him. He forgot about the concerns of the present and lay in the hammock for much of the time, thinking only of the past, of his home in England and of his time on the island. Yet now he found it hard to clearly remember the faces of his mother and father and little sister. They were gradually slipping from focus, and even his memories of Robinson had begun to fade. He forgot about eating and drinking and fell into a semi-wakeful state, listless and apathetic. Almost as if he himself was slipping from focus.

But then, he had a dream.

Not a nightmare, but a dream of deep contentment. He dreamed that instead of lying in a hammock, he was lying in a cradle in the dappled shade of the apple tree beside the grey stone farmhouse where he was born. He was a baby, and was watching butterflies dancing among the leaves above him and listening to the birds singing. It was warm and sunny and though he was quite alone he was perfectly happy.

But then a drop of water fell on his fore-head. And soon, raindrops were falling hard, pitter-patter, all around him.

Had he been awake, rain might have brought hope and joy, but in the dream it brought doubt and fear. The butterflies were gone now, the birds too; Jack could only hear the rain. Louder and louder, splashing down and gradually filling up the cradle with water. He opened his mouth to cry out.

A drop of rain fell upon his tongue.

It was salty.

In an instant, Jack was awake, the dream wiped from his mind. And yet it was still raining.

Water was falling all around him. And it was dark. He could

just make out the awning above, sagging down, stretched like a shirt over a full fat belly, wet and dripping. He reached up and pushed his finger into it. Water ran down his arm as if he had turned on a tap. Seawater.

Jumping down from the hammock, Jack found that the pool of water below was now much deeper, well above his waist, and he could hear water gushing into the bottle above him and splashing down into another pool collecting in the awning. It must have been pouring through the air hole in the cork. The bottle must be down below the surface. It must be sinking.

Quickly, he pulled off his soaking wet shirt and climbed the rope ladder up to where the water spurted like a leak from a pipe. He took one sleeve of the shirt and, while holding the cork in place by pulling on the thread, pushed it up into the hole. The flow of water was reduced to a trickle – momentarily at least. It wouldn't hold. He'd need to push the whole shirt in for it to be at all secure. But the air hole was too narrow for his hand and arm. He climbed partway down the ladder, raised his foot and stamped as hard as he could on one of the sticks wedged across the bottle, supporting the awning. The stick broke with a sharp crack and the awning tipped sideways, spilling water into the pool at the bottom of the bottle. Grabbing one half of the broken stick, he pulled it free of the rope thread, then climbed back up towards the cork. At that moment, the shirt was forced from the air hole and slapped down on top of him. Water gushed down with renewed force. He gathered up the shirt again and began to ram it into the hole as hard as he could, pushing it with the stick until most of it was squashed into the air hole, a tight soggy bung. That was all he could do for the present, though he knew the bung wouldn't hold for very long.

But *why* had water gushed in through the air hole? Why was the bottle sinking?

And why was it so dark?

It didn't *feel* like night. The darkness wasn't that infinite void of blackness that surrounded the bottle in the nighttime. Rather it felt as though something was *blocking out* the light – as though something had *wrapped itself* around the bottle.

At that moment he became aware of a noise. A squeaking, scraping noise, like fingernails scratching against a windowpane.

He climbed down the ladder and, standing in the pool

of seawater, leaned against the side of the bottle, peering out through the glass.

Then he jumped back with a start.

There was something there.

Stuck there. Pushed up against the glass on the outside of the bottle – *moving* – alive!

A great ring of rubbery flesh with a hard toothy edge, almost like a circular mouth, tensing and relaxing, trying to gain purchase.

A giant sucker.

And there were more. They completely enclosed the bottle.

He'd seen them once before – in a rock pool on the island; on the arms of a small octopus.

Some monstrous *many armed* creature had taken hold of the bottle.

A surge of icy fear drenched his body as he recalled Old Ma Rollock once telling him of such a creature. A creature dreaded by all sailors. A creature that could wrap its deadly arms about ships and drag them down to the bottom of the ocean.

The Kraken.

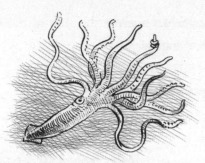

Chapter Forty-Seven
Monsters

The bottle jolted and Jack was thrown down under the water for a moment. A shaft of dim light pierced the gloom above him. The creature had shifted its grip; there was a space between the suckers. He quickly climbed the ladder and looked out through the gap.

In the deep blue water, he could see things moving. Huge things, waving and curling and writhing like the fronds of some giant seaweed swaying in the current.

The arms of the creature.

He looked down and could vaguely make out the shape of the thing's vast body. The bottle was being drawn closer and closer towards it. And suddenly a giant orb with a great black disc at its centre was there, right in front of him, just outside the bottle. A colossal eye. An eye as big as a house

– looking in at Jack with the cold unblinking stare of a creature from another world.

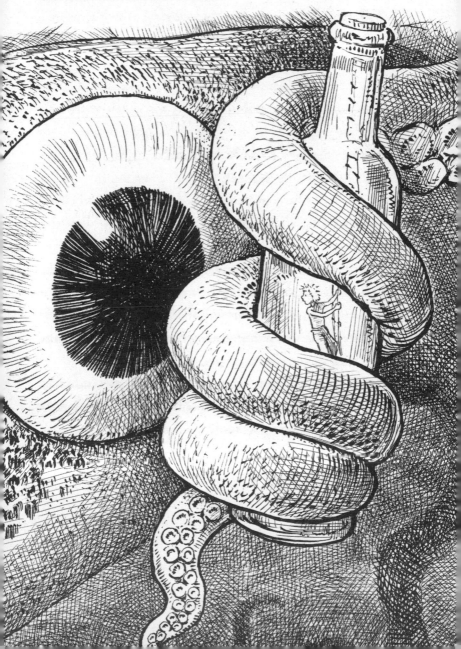

Perhaps the creature wondered if it was worth cracking open this strange shellfish to get at the tiny morsel inside?

Jack never found out. For the eye suddenly disappeared and the bottle was jerked and spun around violently. Briefly, Jack glimpsed a huge gaping maw zooming towards him and filling the whole of his vision before *The Lucky Bottle* was released and shot up and up and up and out into the sky above, like a cork popping from a champagne bottle.

When, finally, it splashed back down again, Jack felt as though he'd left his stomach behind. Even so, he jumped up as quickly as he could and looked into the water below.

Down there, something filled the ocean – filled the entire world, it seemed. An immeasurable creature, which, only as it sank down and down, further and further away from him, did Jack perceive to be a whale.

Its jaws were clamped around the body of a giant squid, while the squid's writhing arms wrapped about the blunt square head of the whale.

Two titans of the deep locked in deadly combat, gradually sinking from view, though even fathoms below, the great whale was still visible, shimmering in the dark blue deep.

For it was milky white.

Chapter Forty-Eight
The Great Storm

The remains of the last ten yummies were floating in the deep pool of seawater that now sloshed around the bottom of the bottle. The sack of yummies had fallen when Jack had broken the stick, and this, and *The Lucky Bottle*'s unexpected 'flight', had loosened the whole of the internal framework completely; it now clattered from side to side with the rise and fall of the waves. Worst of all: the last bottle of fresh water had been smashed.

And yet, bizarrely, Jack was feeling happier than he'd felt for weeks.

He was alive! *Really* alive. Gone was the listless apathy, the indifference to his fate. He was tingling with vitality. And at that moment, he really did feel like the luckiest boy in the whole world.

He climbed the rope ladder, pushed up the cork and leaned out of the bottle, breathing in the fresh air, and feeling utterly elated. A stiff wind ruffled his hair and as he turned to face it, the bottle rose to the top of a wave and he saw, stretched all along the horizon, a line of dark grey clouds.

Racing on the wind, they soon filled half the sky and then, as if a bucket of water had been thrown in his face, Jack felt the first drop of rain.

Quickly, he climbed down the ladder and untied the rain catcher from where he'd secured it above the pool, along with the last unbroken empty bottle, which thankfully he'd kept wrapped up inside the rain catcher and ready for use. Back at the top, he unfurled the catcher so that it sat like a funnel above *The Lucky Bottle*, then held the empty bottle below the small hole at its centre.

One drop would be enough.

The wind, however, had other ideas. It grew stronger, tugging and buffeting the rain catcher like an umbrella on a blustery day, and Jack, gripping one of the wooden struts, found it impossible to hold the thing still. When he did manage to catch a drop of rain, it missed the empty bottle he was holding completely. As the wind grew stronger and

232

the waves bigger and bigger, *The Lucky Bottle* was almost upended. It was all Jack could do to hang on to the catcher and save it from being blown away. He gave up trying to catch rain and, letting go of the bottle, took hold of the catcher with both hands to pull it back inside. But at that moment a great gust caught the rain catcher and lifted it, along with Jack, right out of the bottle . . .

Almost in slow motion, Jack watched in horror as *The Lucky Bottle* receded below his feet. He saw, all around, the mountainous sea; waves like towering snow-capped alps and the troughs between them, deep cavernous valleys. He saw the angry black sky and the swirling sheets of rain. All fury, turmoil and turbulence.

And then, right beside him, he saw the cork, attached to the cotton thread.

Instantly, he released the rain catcher and grabbed the thread. Then, hand over hand, he began to haul himself back towards *The Lucky Bottle*. Completely disoriented, he had no sense of which way up he was, and only when things began flying from the bottle did he realize it must be upside down. And he saw too, that the bottle itself had been tossed into the air now. The loose sticks almost brained him as they flew out of the neck. The hammock, the knife, fragments of broken bottle, all came flying past him. And though he tucked his head between his arms to protect himself, he was cut and bruised and battered – and almost skewered when the fishing spear flew from the bottle. Still, he clung on, hauling himself inch by inch along the cotton thread towards the bottle.

Yet the bottle, instead of getting nearer was getting further and further away from him. The stone was slipping down towards the top of the bottle. If it reached the opening . . .

Clunk!

He felt a jolt as the thread snapped taught; the stone had stuck at the neck of the bottle!

In a flash, he remembered how he and Robinson had had to turn the stone sideways to drop it in – it was oval-shaped and only fitted in one way.

He hauled faster and had just put a hand on the bottle's rim when the dark sky above grew darker still . . . and he looked up.

Rising high to fill half the sky, was a great wave. A wave so big it seemed as if the ocean itself had tipped sideways and the distant horizon was now far, far above him.

In moments, it would come crashing down. A thousand tons of angry water crashing down upon Jack and *The Lucky Bottle*, thrusting them deep under the cold, black sea.

He would surely be smashed to smithereens.

And he certainly would have been . . . if he hadn't hauled himself back into the bottle and pulled the cork firmly into place just in time.

Even so, when that wave crashed upon the bottle – down – down – down it went – deeper – deeper – deeper into the chasm of the ocean – whirling, twirling, twisting, tumbling, spinning through the water, then . . .

Up – up – up – higher – higher – higher – and out into the air on the crest of another wave, tossed into the void, whirling, twirling, twisting, tumbling, spinning across the sky, and splashing down into the sea. Then . . .

Down – down – down again . . .

And more whirling, twirling, twisting, tumbling over and over and over again . . .

Jack was undoubtedly better off in the bottle than out, but if he'd been bouncing around inside it, he would certainly have been battered to pieces. He wasn't, luckily. He was squeezed up in the neck, just under the cork, wedged against the sides and hanging on tightly to the cotton thread . . .

And feeling absolutely wretched again.

There came a point when he felt he could hang on no longer. His grip began to loosen, and gradually he began to slip down the neck of the bottle. But then, mercifully, the whirling, twirling, twisting and tumbling grew gentler and slower, and moments later had ceased altogether. The wind eased, the waves subsided, the clouds lifted, and the sun came out.

The great storm abated.

In reality, it was probably no more than a minor squall, over in a few minutes. However, it certainly *felt* like a great storm to tiny Jack.

Soon, the waves were stilled altogether, and the sea was dead flat calm, as smooth as a polished tabletop.

Utterly exhausted, Jack slid down the cotton thread until he was hanging just above the pool of water. His mind was blank. Drained and shattered, the stark reality of his situation gradually began to dawn upon him.

Everything was gone. Even the rope ladder had become detached in the storm. But for the pool of seawater, the stone and the thread attaching it to the cork, the bottle was empty.

He was surely doomed.

Then he remembered what Robinson had said about his lucky pebble:

'Believe in it, Jack!' he'd said. 'And whenever the whole world seems to have turned against you and everything seems hopeless, put your hand into your pocket and take hold of that lucky pebble, and remember that everything will turn out all right in the end.'

Jack put his right hand into his right trouser pocket.

It was empty.

Chapter Forty-Nine
A Voice

He pulled the inside of the pocket right out. Nothing.
He put his left hand into his left trouser pocket.
Empty.

The lucky pebble was gone.

But worse than this – so were the *bottles*. The red bottle and the green bottle, filled with the magic potions, were gone!

He slid down into the pool, peering under the water, turning this way and that, searching.

There *was* something there. Something lying at the bottom of the bottle that caught the sun and sparkled. He reached down under the water and picked it up.

It was the golden Spanish doubloon.

He began to laugh. A hollow, despairing laugh. Of all

the things in his bottle, this, the most valuable, but the most useless, was all that remained.

There was nothing else.

At that moment he heard a voice.

Not in his head, which was his first thought, but a *real* voice, somewhere outside.

He listened, not quite believing his own ears. It was muffled and indistinct, but unmistakable. Somewhere nearby there must be a boat.

Putting the doubloon in his pocket, with the last of his strength, he pulled himself up the cotton thread to the top of the bottle.

There *was* a boat. He could see it, becalmed, not twenty yards away. A great three-masted galleon with huge square sails hanging still and slack. He braced his feet against the sides of the bottle, put his shoulder to the cork, and pushed. But the cork wouldn't budge. He pushed harder. Still, it wouldn't budge. He'd been hanging on to the thread all through the storm and now the cork was wedged in more tightly than ever. He hadn't the strength to shift it. He was stuck inside the bottle.

Again, he heard the voice, clearer and more distinct now. A strange, squawky voice. It said:

'There's a bottle of rum in the water! There's a bottle of rum in the water!'

Chapter Fifty
Rum

'*There's a bottle of rum in the water!*' squawked Lord Boothby, perched on Bad Bob's shoulder.

Scowling ferociously, the old pirate paced up and down, wooden leg stomping on the deck – *Whack!* – *Whack!* – *Whack!* He was in the darkest of moods and paid no heed to the parrot. Its incessant chatter was now just background noise, and though there had been a time when Bad Bob and all the other pirates had laughed loudly at Lord Boothby's droll little utterances, they didn't any more. The novelty of the bird's speech had long since worn off, and it might as well have been squawking '*Pretty Polly*' or '*Hello, sailor!*' for all the notice they took of it. It never crossed their minds that the parrot ever spoke *sense*.

And yet . . . Bad Bob had heard *something*.

One word had somehow penetrated the captain's consciousness. A word he'd had been brooding on for several days. The cause, indeed, of his black mood. A word that had an exhilarating effect upon the old pirate, sending a thrill of excitement through those limbs he still retained and inducing a desperate thirst that caused his throat to constrict.

The word was '*rum*'.

'WHO SAID THAT?' he bellowed, his wooden leg whacking down so loudly that all the pirates jumped a foot or so into the air.

There was not a drop of rum left on the ship. The kegs were dry, the bottles empty – and yet someone was talking about the golden liquor . . .

Bad Bob's single eye swivelled this way and that, skewering each of the pirates in turn with its piercing gaze.

Stomachs tightened, hearts began to race and sweat glistened on brows. The pirates looked around at one another, bewildered. And then at last, Nobby Nibbs, the first mate, spoke up.

'Who said what, Cap'n?'

Bad Bob fixed him with a savage stare.

'RUM, Master Nibbs. Who said *RUM*? Someone's talkin' about *RUM*!'

Bad Bob scanned the faces of the crew once more, and then, in a voice dripping with malice, said: 'If I find that someone's got a secret stash . . .'

Hands began to tremble and knees to knock as the pirates shook their heads vigorously.

Then, into the baleful silence, Lord Boothby squawked: *'There's a bottle of RUM in the water!'*

And this time, everyone heard what the parrot had said.

They breathed a collective sigh of relief, and Nobby Nibbs cried, "Twas the *bird*, Cap'n! 'Twas only the bird. An' *'e* don't talk sense!'

The pirates began to laugh. Bad Bob, however, remained silent and their laughter soon subsided.

Approaching Nobby Nibbs, the captain raised the hook, worn in place of his missing left hand, and placed its sharp point beneath the first mate's clean-shaven chin . . . then raised it an inch or so. Nobby Nibbs gulped and stretched up his neck as far as it would stretch. The hook pierced the skin, drawing a little blood, and the first mate let out a small squeak. Slowly, Bad Bob turned Nibbs's chin to face the ocean, then raised his right arm, pointing out over the water.

'Don't 'e, Master Nibbs?' the captain said with a wicked smile. *'Don't* 'e talk sense?'

About twenty yards from the ship, floating becalmed on the tranquil ocean, was a bottle . . .

Chapter Fifty-One
Squinty and Sticky

Robinson's mimicry had been perfect. Jack knew exactly to whom that voice belonged. And he knew whose shoulder the bird would be perched upon.

He watched, powerless, as a rowing boat was lowered from the ship and two pirates climbed down to sit within it, one at the oars and one at the bow. The boat approached.

He pushed and pushed, but still the cork wouldn't budge. He took the thread connecting cork and stone in his mouth and tried to bite through it, chewing as hard as he could. But it was no good; it was like trying to bite through a thick rope.

And now the rowing boat was there, alongside the bottle . . .

A hand reached down; fingers wrapped around the bottle's neck enclosing him in darkness.

The bottle was lifted from the ocean . . .

"Ere, Squinty – there's somethin' in there!' cried Sticky Tom, as he reached down a long – stick-like – arm and grabbed the bottle.

'Why sure there is, Sticky – there's *rum* in there, i'nt there?' replied Squinty-Eyed Jake, sitting at the oars with his back to Sticky Tom.

'Nah, Squinty, somethin' *else*. Look at that!' He tipped the bottle from side to side and the stone on the thread, slid from side to side, banging gently against the glass – clunk – clunk – clunk. Squinty-Eyed Jake half turned and screwed up his eyes. Then shook his head.

'Can't see nothin'. Hand it over.' He was very short- sighted.

Sticky Tom passed him the bottle and he held it in front of his face, three inches from his right eye.

'Ah ha! Now I see it!' he exclaimed. 'A stone on a thread! What's that doin' in there then?'

Slowly, he raised his head, his eye following the thread up towards the cork.

'Uh! What's *that*?' he said, peering even more closely.

'What?'

'There's somethin' *else* in there, Sticky! Somethin' . . . *alive*. I saw it move!'

Sticky Tom reached an arm over Squinty-Eyed Jake's shoulder.

'Let's 'ave a look! Let's 'ave a look!'

'Leave orf!' growled Squinty-Eyed Jake, holding the bottle at arm's length, and pushing away Sticky Tom's hand. '*I'm* still lookin'!'

He screwed his eye up even tighter and held the bottle even closer.

For the second time that day, an eye looked in at Jack. This one wasn't anywhere near so large as the first and only just visible between wrinkles of eyelid and hairy brow, but was still no less disconcerting. Jack tried to keep as still as possible, though his arms and legs ached unbearably.

The eye blinked.

'There's a little *creature* in there!' cried Squinty-Eyed Jake, and then, in a bemused voice, 'An' it *looks* like . . . Nah, can't be. Must be a crab . . . Yeah, that's what it is. A crab's got in there. So, it can't be rum – must be seawater.'

Sticky Tom stood up and leaned over Squinty-Eyed Jake's shoulder.

'Let's see it then. Show us! Show us!'

Squinty-Eyed Jake was just about to hand the bottle to Sticky Tom when a great bellow boomed across from the ship.

'WHAT ARE YOU DOIN' WITH MY RUM? PUT THAT BOTTLE DOWN *NOW*! AND GET BACK HERE SHARPISH!'

Chapter Fifty-Two

Drunk!

Squinty-Eyed Jake quickly laid the bottle on the bottom boards and took up the oars.

'Look lively, lads!' ordered Nobby Nibbs, as the boat drew up alongside the ship. 'Toss up that bottle!'

''Fraid t'ain't rum, Cap'n,' said Squinty-Eyed Jake as he tossed the bottle up to the first mate. 'Jus' seawater.'

'*Seawater*, is it?' roared Bad Bob, grasping the bottle by the neck and holding it aloft. 'An' 'ow do you know that Mister Squinty? Been tastin' it 'ave you?'

'Oh no, Cap'n! Ain't touched a drop. But there's somethin' inside there. There's –'

'*Somethin'* inside, is there?' interrupted the captain, swinging the bottle from side to side and watching the stone clunk against the glass.

Lord Boothby tipped his head along with the bottle, his beady eyes fixed upon the stone.

'Yes, Cap'n,' replied the short-sighted oarsman as he clambered back on board. 'There's . . .'

'A STONE!' bellowed Bad Bob, fixing a fearsome eye upon Squinty-Eyed Jake. 'I may only have *one*, Mister Squinty,' growled the captain. 'But it's a better eye than *both* o' yours!'

The oarsman quailed and remained silent.

'Now, *why* is there a stone in there, Mister Squinty? A stone tied to a thread and attached to the cork? Can you answer me *that*?'

Squinty-Eyed Jake opened and closed his mouth several times, then shook his head. 'No, Cap'n.'

'Do you see the cork, Mister Squinty?'

The bottle's top was visible above the grip of Bad Bob's hand, and Squinty-Eyed Jake, stepping forward nervously, peered closely at it.

'Yes, sir, Cap'n, I can see the cork, but . . .'

'GOOD!' interrupted Bad Bob. 'Now, look closely, Mister Squinty. Do you see that it's not a *whole* cork, but just a small *part* o' one?'

The oarsman nodded. 'Yes, Cap'n, but . . .'

'AND . . . a small *part* of a cork ain't nearly so secure as a *whole* one, is it?'

'No, Cap'n, but . . .'

'SO . . . perhaps that stone is there to keep that cork

250

securely in place, Mister Squinty. Do you think that might be the case?'

'Er, yes, Cap'n, but . . .'

'AND . . . *why* would someone do that – if it's just *seawater* in there?'

'Er, dunno, Cap'n, but . . .'

'NO MORE *BUTS!* HOLD YOUR TONGUE, MISTER SQUINTY, OR I'LL CUT IT OUT AND FEED IT TO THE BIRD!'

'*Cut it out! Cut it out!*' squawked Lord Boothby excitedly, hopping from one foot to the other.

Squinty-Eyed Jake closed his mouth quickly.

Bad Bob raised the bottle up to the light and the sun's rays shone through the golden amber liquid within.

'Is *that* the colour of seawater, Mister Squinty?' asked the captain.

The oarsman shook his head.

'No, indeed, Mister Squinty. It's the colour of *RUM!*'

It was. The residue of the mushy brown yummies had tainted the water and turned it the exact colour of rum.

The captain raised the bottle, gripped the cork between crooked, blackened teeth and jerked it out. The stone rose and jammed at the neck, the thread tightened, then snapped and the stone dropped – *clunk* – to the bottom of the bottle. And with a little splash, something else fell into the amber liquid . . .

Bad Bob spat out the cork and raised the bottle once

more, then Lord Boothby squawked:

'There's a little man in there! There's a little man in there!'

Then:

'Too late, you drank 'im!'

Chapter Fifty-Three

Spat!

Bad Bob had drained the whole bottle before realizing that Squinty-Eyed Jake was dead right; it *was* seawater.

And now it sloshed around between his rotten teeth like the tide about the stumps of an old pier, along with the residue of rancid food, old fish bones and the oozy pus from mouth ulcers . . . and Jack too, of course, half-drowned, swirling around like flotsam in a whirlpool, drawn ever closer to the great black hole that was Bad Bob's gullet . . .

Just in time, Jack grabbed hold of a stump of tooth to raise his head and gulp in a lungful of air.

Except it *wasn't* air. It was Bad Bob's foul breath. Jack retched and, losing his hold on the tooth, was sucked once more into the seething, noxious tide . . .

Then Bad Bob spat.

Violently.

Over the side of the ship.

And then, to the frank astonishment of the other pirates, Squinty-Eyed Jake was foolhardy enough to venture:

'*Seawater*, Cap'n?'

Bad Bob stared, his face colouring to a thunderous shade of purple, then roared. And the blast of that roar was such that the mainsail billowed as if caught by a mighty gust of wind . . . and the ship shifted slightly. Then – *WHACK!* – the captain's wooden leg came down with such force, timbers shuddered, and several pirates lost their balance and fell to the deck.

Squinty-Eyed Jake turned very pale . . .

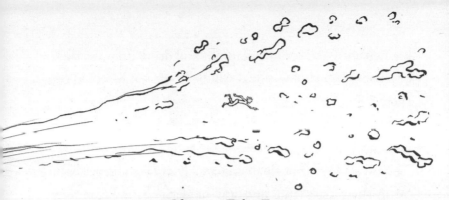

Chapter Fifty-Four
Tiger Stripes

J ack was shot from that mouth like a pea from a pea-shooter, zooming through the air and dropping down into the ocean yards and yards from the ship (quite unharmed, thankfully, for small things fall much more lightly than large heavy ones).

Even so, he was now in a far worse predicament than any he'd yet faced. He'd escaped the horrors of that appalling mouth, but he was alone in the ocean without even an empty bottle to sail in. He was surely doomed

Yet, strangely, he was not without hope.

There *was* a chance. A very small one. And even if he was destined to remain beetle-sized for the rest of his life in a hostile world where spiders and wasps would be terrifying monsters, and where he'd sleep in a matchbox on the kitchen shelf and eat breadcrumbs and drink from the shell of an acorn . . . home would still be home – if he could get there.

He turned and looked up at the ship, looming like a great dark island silhouetted against the late afternoon sky. That was where that small chance lay. If he could get back on to the pirates' ship and stay hidden – a tiny stowaway – there'd be a chance that when the ship put into a port somewhere he'd be able to find another ship that could take him back to England – or at least to another, larger port.

He kicked his feet and had just begun swimming towards the ship when suddenly, a thunderous roar reverberated through the air, sending a shiver of vibration across the surface of the ocean. It was followed by a tremendous *THWACK!* and then by the rasping sound of a cutlass being drawn from a belt. Then:

'Cut it out! Cut it out!'

Undaunted, Jack continued to swim.

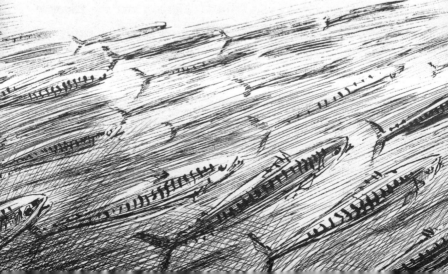

A few yards is not much of a distance. But to Jack, weary to the point where his whole body ached, the ship was as good as a mile away. He swam slowly. Waves of any size would have made his task impossible, but fortunately the sea remained as flat as a pancake, and in due course he reached the deep shadow cast by the galleon. He would be less visible now; hidden, he hoped, from the beady eye of that clever parrot. The cliff-like side of the ship loomed close, and he was just beginning to wonder how on earth he'd climb aboard, when a movement in the water below caught his eye. For a horrifying second, he thought it might be a tentacle of that squid again, reaching up towards him.

But it wasn't a squid.

Looking fathoms down into the crystal-clear water, he saw dark shapes. Blue-green tiger-striped shapes, moving fast. He knew immediately what they were.

One of the mackerel turned with a flash of silver and turquoise and began speeding towards him. Another turned, and then another. Gripped by panic, he swam frantically – flailing, kicking, thrashing wildly, like a floundering moth trapped on the surface of a pond. The mackerel shot through the water like torpedoes – the whole shoal zooming up now, beady eyes fixed upon him, hungry mouths wide open . . .

Then he hit something.

Something hard and smooth and shiny.

The bottle! Bad Bob must have tossed it overboard!

If he could get back into *The Lucky Bottle*, he'd be safe! He grabbed at the glass, trying to gain some grip . . . but of course, it was impossible.

The mackerel were close now . . . Then something splashed down into the water beside him. The cork! The cork attached to the thread. He grabbed the thread and pulled himself up on to the cork. And suddenly – amazingly, *miraculously* – the cork was lifted out of the ocean and up and up and up the side of the bottle, and the mackerel were jumping, snapping at the cork, but he was almost at the top of the bottle now and . . .

There was someone there, hauling on the thread.

Eyes sparkling with joy, and teeth spread into a wide grin, gleaming from within a great black beard . . .

Chapter Fifty-Five

The Glimmer of Hope

'Robinson!' cried Jack, flinging his arms around Robinson's neck, his face pressed into the great black beard. He burst into tears.

The mackerel were still jumping high and snapping all around them as Robinson quickly lifted Jack into the bottle and, once inside, pulled the cork into place above them. Cradling Jack with one arm, he climbed down the rope ladder.

'Oh, Robinson, Robinson,' cried Jack, between tears and laughter. 'I thought I would never see you again!'

'Me too!' laughed Robinson. He put Jack down and handed him a bottle of water. 'Drink,' he commanded.

Jack drank. He drank almost half the bottle before pausing to gulp in a few deep breaths. Then he blurted, 'I lost

my pebble, Robinson! And I lost the magic potions! I lost *everything*! And there was a *monster*, and then *he* nearly swallowed me – Bad Bob! And . . .' He stopped, out of breath.

'I know, Jack, I know!' said Robinson, nodding. 'About Bad Bob, at least. I was here all the time, listening to all that was happening, frantically wondering what I could possibly do to save you!'

Jack wiped the tears from his cheeks with the back of his hand, then frowned. 'But *how*? How are you here? Is it magic? You are *real*, aren't you, Robinson? I'm not dreaming, am I?'

'No, I'm real,' laughed Robinson. 'And I only used the same magic that you used, Jack. And had a bit of luck! I got caught in a storm that must have helped me catch you up.'

'The same magic? Why yes, you're *small*, Robinson, like

me! But how did you get into *The Lucky Bottle?*'

'This isn't *The Lucky Bottle*, Jack. This is *my* bottle. I've called it *The Glimmer of Hope.*'

Jack looked around and realized that of course it couldn't be *The Lucky Bottle*. There was a rope ladder, and water bottles, and there were still some yummies and a rain catcher and a fishing spear, and there was a wooden structure too, arranged just the way Jack had arranged his, with a hammock and awning.

'You look very *thin*, Jack,' said Robinson. 'You'd better eat.' He handed Jack a yummy, which he devoured greedily.

Outside, the mackerel were swimming around and around the bottle, staring in at Jack and Robinson with wild hungry eyes.

'Have another,' said Robinson, holding up a second fruit when Jack had almost finished the first. Jack was about to take it when he saw how few there were left and saw how gaunt and hollow-eyed Robinson looked. He must have been starving himself.

'I'm fine, Robinson,' he said. 'But why *The Glimmer of Hope*?'

'Because that's all I had, Jack – just a glimmer of hope that I'd ever find you! But wonder of wonders . . . here you are!'

'But how did you know to come and save me?'

Robinson shook his head. 'I should never have let you go. I knew I'd made a terrible mistake the moment your bottle disappeared among the waves. I was a fool. I realized immediately that I'd have to follow you – no matter how small a chance there was that I'd ever find you.'

'But, Robinson – your *island*!' cried Jack in dismay. 'With all your wonderful books and everything! You were happy – you didn't want to live anywhere else . . .'

'Nonsense, Jack, that life wasn't worth a fig! Not once you'd gone.'

Jack burst into tears – tears of real distress.

'Dear me, dear me. Don't cry so. I really mean it; that old life *wasn't* worth a fig. I may have found a kind of happiness on the island once, but when I watched your bottle disappearing among the waves, Jack, I knew I could never be happy again. I'd lost the one thing – the *only* thing – that made my life worth living. I'd lost a friend, Jack! The one and only friend I ever had in my whole life! I'd thought

I could find all the friends I ever needed in books, but the greatest lesson I learned from stories was that I was wrong. They taught me about life, Jack; they softened my heart to the rest of mankind and taught me how to *feel*. But I wasn't *really* happy until I met you. And all the books in all the libraries in all the world aren't worth tuppence when set against friendship, Jack.

'And then what did I do? I sent my only friend sailing across the ocean in a *bottle*!'

Jack looked utterly forlorn.

'Oh, Robinson, I'm so sorry! I've been so selfish; I've only ever thought of what *I* wanted. And now you've lost everything and it's all my fault!'

'Don't give it another thought, Jack. Honestly. Seeing you rising up the side of the bottle just now, sitting on that cork, was the happiest moment of my entire life! And that feeling was worth any number of dusty old books! Don't be downhearted – I'm not!'

Jack smiled weakly. 'But they weren't just dusty old books, Robinson. And now you've lost them all.'

'Not *all*. I brought two along with me. I probably shouldn't have, I should have brought more supplies, but I couldn't resist.' He reached over and, picking up a rough canvas bag, withdrew a tightly wrapped bundle of sailcloth. 'I won't unwrap it,' he said. 'The smell would be quite over-powering in here! But this is the book of spells. And I also brought this one – the book that led me to the island, *The*

Tempest – my lucky talisman!'

At the mention of luck, Jack asked, 'But, Robinson – however *did* you find me? It was surely an impossible thing to do – harder than finding a needle in a haystack. You said you had just a glimmer of hope, but how could you have had *any?*'

'Well, I also had a little bit of *luck.*'

He reached inside his right trouser pocket and took out a small, shiny black pebble.

Chapter Fifty-Six
The Harpoon

'**M**y lucky pebble!' cried Jack. 'But, Robinson . . . it was at the bottom of the ocean!'

'It wasn't,' laughed Robinson. 'You never took it with you, Jack. You dropped it on the beach before you ever set off! It must have fallen out of your pocket somehow, when you were putting in and taking out the potions. Hercules spotted it – the noble, sharp-eyed beast – and thank goodness he did!'

He lifted Jack's hand and placed the pebble on his palm.

'Put it back into your pocket, Jack, and keep it safe!'

Jack put the lucky pebble back into his pocket but was suddenly distressed once more. 'But I lost the potions, Robinson!' he cried. 'I lost the antidote to make me big again!'

'Don't worry, Jack, I still have *my* potions, and there's plenty for both of us and a good many others besides.'

To reassure Jack, he took the bottles from his pockets – clear bottles, filled with the vivid-green yummy-juice potions. Each had a label tied around the neck. On one was the word 'BIG', and on the other, 'SMALL'.

At that moment, a roar came blasting out from the ship above.

'FIND 'IM! FIND THE SQUINTY-EYED SCOUNDREL AND BRING 'IM 'ERE!'

Squinty-Eyed Jake must have fled from the deck and be hiding somewhere.

Robinson stuffed the potions back in his pockets with a sudden air of urgency.

'You'll have to tell me all about your adventures another time, Jack. And I'll tell you about how I managed to shrink myself and get into this bottle while up to my neck in the sea – a rather ticklish operation! But right now, we need to do something about getting away from here!'

He climbed the rope ladder, and Jack followed, squeezing up beside him after he'd pushed out the cork. Rising high above them, just a few feet away, was the great galleon.

Jack suddenly frowned. 'Why didn't the pirates see *your* bottle, Robinson?' he said, 'It's much closer to the ship.'

'I think that's exactly why they *didn't* see it, Jack. It lies in the shadow of the ship and must be almost invisible when looking from bright sunlight into the darkness. That, however, is about to change. The sun will soon be creeping round above the stern and this bottle will be caught in its rays and shining out like a beacon. We need to get away from here very soon.'

He raised his arm and pointed to the rowing boat, which was still tied up alongside the galleon.

'*That's* our only chance.'

'What? The rowing boat?'

'Precisely, Jack. There's not a breath of wind to fill the sails of the ship, but that boat has *oars*! Right now, it's the only thing capable of going anywhere.'

'But it's huge, Robinson. How would we . . . Oh, you mean we'd *shrink* it?'

'Not at all, Jack. That would be no good. A tiny rowing boat wouldn't stand a chance among waves of any size. I think now is the time for us to become big again!'

'But . . . but what about the pirates? They are sure to see us if we're big.'

'Not necessarily, Jack. The pirates seem to be rather pre-occupied just now.'

They could hear Bad Bob grumbling away like a rumbling volcano, his wooden leg thwacking the deck as he paced up and down impatiently.

'If we're quiet, and lucky,' continued Robinson, 'we could get away without being spotted. And once away, they'll not be able to follow us. Unless, of course, they have another boat, which is quite possible. But even then, I'm pretty

267

handy with a pair of oars and I suspect their best oarsman is indisposed at present! I think the odds are with us.'

Jack nodded. This all made perfect sense.

'So, are we going to do it now? Make ourselves big?'

'Not right here,' said Robinson. 'That wouldn't be a good idea. We can't do it *inside* the bottle of course – that could be very nasty – and if we did it standing on the rim there would certainly be a fair amount of splashing as we fell into the ocean. The pirates would be sure to notice that. I think we need to wait until we're in the boat. The only problem is getting there.'

Jack looked down into the ocean.

'The mackerel are gone,' he said. 'We could swim, couldn't we? It's not that far.'

Robinson shook his head. 'No, I don't think that's a good idea.'

'Why not?'

'It's just not.' He sounded a little embarrassed.

'But why not, Robinson? How else are we going to get there?'

'It's not a good idea because I *can't swim!*'

'You can't?'

'No, I can't!'

'Oh,' said Jack, a little incredulous. 'You mean you lived on that island, surrounded by the ocean, for all that time and yet never learned to swim?'

Robinson was silent.

'I think you are going to have to learn, Robinson – and very quickly!'

'No, Jack – I have a better idea!' Robinson disappeared into the bottle and reappeared a moment later carrying a long, thin piece of shiny metal. At one end was a sharp point, and at the other, a thin, slit-like opening.

'Your needle!' cried Jack.

'My needle? Why, no. My *harpoon!*'

Chapter Fifty-Seven
Getting Big Again

The sun was just above the stern of the galleon as Robinson tied a thread to the eye of the needle-harpoon and climbed up on to the rim of the bottle. Holding it in his right hand and bracing his feet on either side of the opening, he reached backwards to the full stretch of his arm and said – 'Watch out for the thread, Jack, it'll come shooting out very fast!' – then he hurled the needle-harpoon forwards, over his shoulder, almost overbalancing and falling into the ocean. Such was the power of Robinson's arm that it flew, straight and true, like a dart from a blow-pipe, towards the gunwale at the top of the rowing boat and stuck there. The thread fell and lay snaking across the ocean between bottle and boat.

Jack was open-mouthed in awe at Robinson's throw.

'Let's see if it holds,' said Robinson as he began hauling on the thread until it was a taut straight line between himself and the needle-harpoon. It held. Very, very slowly the bottle began to move, inch by inch, towards the rowing boat. After five minutes, they were right beside the boat, directly below the needle-harpoon.

'Now we must climb,' said Robinson.

Jack's heart quailed as he looked at the thread, stretching up to the needle-harpoon far above. He'd never be able to climb all that way, he hadn't the strength left. But then Robinson said, 'I'll go first, Jack. Once up there I'll pull you up. No need for you to climb – just hang on.'

Robinson began to climb, reaching arm over arm and clutching the thread between his thighs and feet. In a few minutes, he'd reached the needle-harpoon and pulled himself up on to the gunwale. He signalled down to Jack, and Jack gripped the thread between thighs and feet and held it with both hands. He'd been a sailor too, of course, and knew how to climb a rope. But now he just hung on as

271

tightly as he could as Robinson hauled him up.

The muscles in his arms and legs were trembling like jelly by the time Robinson caught him by the wrist and pulled him up on to the gunwale. For several minutes he sat gasping in lungfuls of air, and Robinson, too, seemed to be exhausted. Presently he said, 'No good getting big here. We'd tip the boat and fall into the ocean. Better do it down *there*.' He pointed into the well of the boat, between the thwarts.

Reaching over the side, he caught hold of the hanging thread and began to pull it up out of the bottle below and toss it over his shoulder into the boat. Once all of it was trailing over the side down to a coiled heap in the well, he said, 'Climb on to my back, Jack, and hang on.'

Jack did, and Robinson, holding the thread and feeding it out above him, began to climb down one of the boat's ribs, abseiling like a climber down a cliff. The rib curved as it descended, gradually becoming less and less steep until eventually there was no need for Robinson to hold the thread and he was soon standing in the middle of the rowing boat, just below the centre thwart. Jack jumped down from his back and Robinson reached into his pocket and took out the bottle of potion with the 'BIG' label.

'Ready?' he said.

Jack nodded.

Pulling out the cork, Robinson lifted the bottle above Jack's head and tipped it very gently. As soon as a drop of the potion fell, he began to chant.

'*Ymmuy ymmuy ymmur ymmur . . .*'

It sounded completely preposterous . . . but it began to work almost immediately.

Jack felt a strange sensation in his tummy. More uncomfortable than the butterflies he'd felt when being shrunk. As though his stomach was being blown up with a pump. It *was* being blown up. He could see it, stretching the waistband of his trousers and inflating like a balloon. He feared he might *pop*.

His arms and legs were puffing up too, and he could feel the seams of his trousers beginning to split. But soon, they too began to grow bigger. The magic must work from the inside out; his clothes were affected last. Eventually, all things had assumed their proper balance and he was big again.

At his feet, Robinson was no larger than a beetle.

'Are you all right?' squeaked the tiny figure.

'I'M FINE!' replied Jack, forgetting that he should whisper now that he was big.

Robinson put a finger to his lips and Jack quickly looked up over his shoulder. But there were no pirates visible above him, and he could still hear Bad Bob, growling and grumbling and stomping about the deck. He could also hear the pleading, desperate voice of Squinty-Eyed Jake:

'Weren't me, Cap'n! I never filled it with water! Weren't me!'

'*Give us your tongue! Give us your tongue!*' squawked Lord Boothby.

Robinson was growing larger now – *inflating*, just as Jack had done. Indeed, he was almost *spherical* and the buttons on his shirt popped off one by one. It looked certain that Robinson must burst. But he didn't, and soon all his various parts had returned to their correct proportions, and he stood beside Jack restored to his normal prodigious size.

They both sat down on the centre thwart and Robinson whispered, 'Now we just need to cut the rope tying the boat to the ship . . .' He paused, then said, 'Oh heck! I've left the knife in the bottle!'

Without a word, Jack leaned over the side and lifted *The Glimmer of Hope* from the water. He tipped it up and shook it gently until all the loose things inside lay on the seat between him and Robinson.

'There!' exclaimed Robinson in an urgent whisper. Jack carefully separated a tiny sparkle of silver from the rest of the pile and moments later the knife – back to its correct size – was in Robinson's hand. But before he could begin to cut the rope there came from above . . . a sharp intake of breath.

They looked up.

Leaning over the side of the ship . . .

staring down at them . . .

was a pirate . . .

Chapter Fifty-Eight

Robinson's Beard

A deep frown crumpled Nobby Nibbs's leathery brow as he gaped in astonishment.

A moment later a second pirate appeared beside him, then a third, and a fourth, and with each successive pirate, came a gasp of startled exclamation as they looked down with astonishment upon the two figures in the rowing boat below. Soon a whole line of gawping pirates had materialized, ranged along the ship's gunwale above.

Their amazement, however, was not, as one might've expected, at the seemingly miraculous appearance, as if from nowhere, of an enormous man and a small boy . . . but at Robinson's *beard*.

And then, from somewhere on the far side of the deck, came their captain's voice:

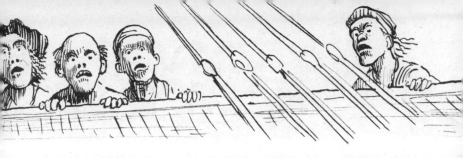

"'Ere, what's up with you lot?'

And then the – *Whack! – Whack! – Whack!* – of the approaching wooden leg . . .

Robinson tried frantically to cut the rope. But the knife was blunt; Jack had taken the best one. This one made painfully slow progress, sawing through the strands.

Whack! – Whack! – Whack!

'*Hurry up! Hurry up!*' pleaded Jack, tugging at Robinson's shirt. But the rope was still more than half intact when the *whacking* ceased.

Jack and Robinson looked up.

The massive figure of Bad Bob towered above the heads of the other pirates. His left arm was raised high, with a whimpering Squinty-Eyed Jake dangling by the collar from the hook at its end, a cutlass blade at his throat.

Bad Bob looked down upon Jack and Robinson . . .

And upon Robinson's *beard*.

Lord Boothby began to hop up and down excitedly on his right shoulder, squawking 'A *beard!* A *beard!* A *beard!*' and Bad Bob's face began to turn a dark shade of

lurid pink with brilliant redder
patches flaring on his cheeks; the
veins at his temples stood out a
violent mauve, and began to
throb, while his mouth twisted
into a manic grin, and a line
of spittle dribbled down his naked
chin . . .

With a flick of his arm, he tossed aside the short-sighted
oarsman and slammed his hook into the gunwale. Then,
lifting his wooden leg, he prepared to leap straight down
into the rowing boat.

But at that moment, Robinson pulled something from
his pocket and held it up high above his head.

It was a little fragment of paper.

Bad Bob froze.

He stared at the fragment of paper.

He stared in particular at the torn, jagged edge of the
little fragment.

His beady eye widened. He'd stared at the mirror image
of that torn jagged edge for so many
hours – for so many *days* – it was now
imprinted indelibly on his mind's
eye.

He dropped his cutlass to
the deck. He raised his right
hand and slid it inside his

coat, withdrawing a larger piece
of paper and deftly unfolding it.

'Nibbs!' he commanded in a
hushed voice, almost trembling
with anticipation. 'Fetch up that
paper!'

The first mate quickly climbed
part way down the side of the ship
and grabbed the fragment from
Robinson's hand, before climbing back up and over the
gunwale.

'Hold it up! Hold it up!' ordered Bad Bob, impatiently.

Nobby Nibbs held up the fragment of paper.

Bad Bob raised his larger sheet and fitted it to the
missing corner. Then he leaned in close . . .

At first, he silently mouthed the words he read on the
reunited parts of the sheet.

A baffled frown creased his brow. Then:

'On – the – shell – of – the – tortoise,' he whispered.
And then again, louder, 'On the shell of the *tortoise*!' And
then finally he bellowed:

'ON THE SHELL OF THE *TORTOISE*! What's that
about then?'

He glared ferociously down at Robinson.

'The map!' declared Robinson, with a beaming smile.
'The *treasure* map is on the shell of the tortoise, most
infamous and illustrious Captain!'

Bad Bob continued to glare.

'And what *tortoise* would that be?'

'Why, the giant tortoise that inhabits the island,' replied Robinson.

For a moment, Bad Bob glared on, then he said, 'And . . . you know where it is then?'

'We do, Captain!' assured Robinson. 'We can take you there.'

A broad smile began to widen across Bad Bob's face. But then he seemed to have second thoughts, and it was replaced by a scowl.

'How do I know that's not just a pack o' lies?' he growled.

Jack quickly reached into his pocket, pulled out the Spanish doubloon and tossed it up towards Nobby Nibbs and Bad Bob. Nobby Nibbs reached out his left hand and caught it, and opening his palm, he held it up before Bad Bob.

'*Red Roger's treasure! Red Roger's treasure!*' squawked Lord Boothby, straining his scrawny neck down towards Nobby Nibbs's palm.

Bad Bob stuffed the paper he was holding into his pocket and picked up the coin. It sparkled red-gold in the last rays of the setting sun. He grinned. Then he noticed something else: written on the fragment of paper that Nobby Nibbs was still holding, he saw the numbers written in the top corner; the exact latitude and longitude of the small rocky island where the treasure was buried. Baring his rotten teeth with a wicked smile, he looked down again at Robinson.

'Don't need for you to take me there, Mister,' he said. And then, to the other pirates, 'Get down there, lads, and take off that BEARD – from the neck up!'

Twenty pirates withdrew their cutlasses from their belts as one and prepared to leap over the gunwale.

But . . .

'*This* beard?' said Robinson, his voice ringing out like the tolling of a great bell, deep and resonant. 'This *brand-new* beard? This whiskery wonder, this bushy profusion that is but the growth of *just one day?*'

And so surprising was this utterance, and so arresting his voice, all the pirates paused, legs astride the gunwale.

Jack's mouth dropped open. He wondered what on earth Robinson was doing; had he gone mad?

But Robinson hadn't finished.

'Am I to lose it so soon?' he continued. 'This beard, so long desired, adorning my previously barren chin and only acquired by means of a *wondrous potion?*'

Still the pirates paused, baffled, and yet somehow bewitched by Robinson's curious speech. At last, however, indignation overcame their bewitchment, and they began to stir.

But Bad Bob didn't move.

'WAIT!' he bellowed, and all the pirates froze once more.

An extraordinary notion had arisen into Bad Bob's consciousness. Planted there, perhaps, by Robinson's words. The idea that his passionate hatred of beards was indeed the result of an intense *jealous*y of those who could grow them. A jealousy stemming, no doubt, from a fervent *desire* to have a beard of his own. For what is a pirate without a beard? A vision sprang into his mind – of himself, standing at the helm, a great black beard jutting proudly from his chin . . .

'Potion?' he growled, suspiciously.

'Indeed!' declared Robinson, taking from his pocket a small bottle filled with vivid-green liquid. He tossed it up towards Bad Bob, who dropped the doubloon, reached out his hand and caught it.

He looked at it, wondering why it was so green and why a label was attached to its neck, bearing the word, SMALL. Doubts began to creep into his mind. But what if it was true?

'One day?' he growled.

'Most certainly,' assured Robinson. 'Sooner perhaps. You will begin to feel the prickle of stubble almost immediately!'

Bad Bob lifted the bottle to his mouth and, gripping the cork between his teeth, pulled it out and spat it over the side of the ship.

Lord Boothby tilted his scrawny head to one side, examining the contents of the bottle with extreme suspicion. Suddenly he squawked:

"E's a liar! 'E's a liar!'

But it was too late.

A smell had risen from the open bottle and gone straight up into Bad Bob's nostrils . . .

'RUM!' he bellowed, turning to face the knot of bewildered pirates who'd gathered beside him. 'Funny colour – but it's *RUM!'*

And putting the bottle to his lips, he took a great gulping mouthful of the vivid-green liquid.

Chapter Fifty-Nine

Something Really Amazing

I t may have *smelled* like rum.

It didn't *taste* like it.

An altogether different flavour masked any trace of the spirit. A flavour so intensely powerful, it shocked Bad Bob's body rigid. His hair stood on end and his eye nearly popped out of his head.

Inside that small innocuous-looking bottle was the concentrated essence, the distilled *awfulness*, of more than thirty yummies; preserved in their foulest, most appalling, bright-green ripeness by the rum and the stopper. The most disgusting, repellent, abominable taste imaginable.

And Bad Bob had drunk almost all of it.

His face nearly exploded!

And he spat!

'YEEEEUUUUCCCCKKKK!'

All over the other pirates . . .

Nobby Nibbs, standing closest, got it full in the face – *SPLAT!* – but no one escaped – it was a very large mouthful, and there were generous helpings for all. Even Sticky Tom, right at the back, got a good smattering of the stuff. And Bad Bob was such a mighty spitter that gobbets of the loathsome potion were sprayed all over the ship. Even Lord Boothby, craning his head to see what was happening to his master's face, got an eyeful.

And then a roar exploded from Bad Bob's wide-open mouth.

'RAAAAAAAAAAAAAAA . . .'

Like the blast of a mighty foghorn, on and on and on, obliterating all other sounds, for Bad Bob had a huge pair of lungs and a vast amount of puff.

If he *hadn't* been roaring, the pirates might have heard another sound – coming from the rowing boat below:

'*Rum rum yummy yum rummy rummy yummy yummy . . .*'

And while Robinson recited the magic spell, Jack was sawing at the rope with the knife. The moment the last strands were parted . . . the spell began to work.

The pirates' galleon began to shrink.

Ropes, rigging, masts, sails – *everything!* – began to shrink. And the pirates too, of course – Bad Bob and Nobby Nibbs and Sticky Tom and Squinty-Eyed Jake and Mr Whelk the cook and Curly Pete and Sid the Skull and all the rest . . . began to shrink. Lord Boothby too, sitting on Bad Bob's shoulder still squawking, '*Liar! Liar! Liar!*' . . . began to shrink.

Bad Bob's roar began to shrink also, diminishing rapidly and sounding like air escaping from a balloon, fizzling away into a tiny little squeak – smaller . . . and smaller . . . and smaller.

Yet it wasn't until Sticky Tom looked up and saw a seagull flying past, that the pirates realized that something very strange was happening.

'Blimey!' he cried. 'What's *that!*'

And all the pirates stopped wiping the nasty green liquid

from their faces and clothes and looked up . . .

A bird far larger than the ship flew above them.

They began to scream and yell and bawl.

And then they saw, looming even larger, two giants, sitting in a gigantic rowing boat . . . and they began to

shriek and howl and wail.

What nightmarish world had they drifted into?

Within seconds all was madness and mayhem. Poor Mr Whelk fainted and tumbled to the deck like a felled tree, causing several of the other pirates to trip over his prone body. Others slipped and skidded on gobbets of the slimy green liquid and soon a great heap of fallen pirates were crawling over one another trying to scramble to their feet, cursing and shouting and squealing . . .

Only one remained standing, unperturbed, and seemingly unaware of the pandemonium all around him: Bad Bob.

He was staring straight ahead, almost in a trance, a smile of blissful rapture spread across his face.

Something amazing was happening. Something *really* amazing.

He'd begun to feel the prickle of *stubble* . . .

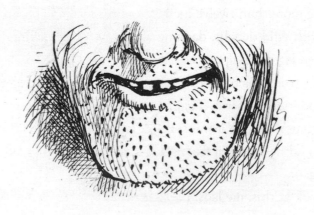

Chapter Sixty

The Abominable Beard

Raising his hand, he stroked his chin.

A beard had begun to grow!

Hairs pricked his palm and within seconds, were pushing through the cracks between his fingers. Thick, black, curly hairs. In moments, the beard was full and bushy, jutting more than twelve inches from his face. He began to yell with wild delight, dancing a clumsy jig, whacking his wooden leg down upon the deck.

"Tis true! 'Tis true!" he cried. 'The potion is a wonder!'

And indeed, it was. That beard had only just begun . . .

In half a minute it was sprawling down across Bad Bob's belly, and he swung it from side to side, as if waving a flag, crying:

'Look at this, me lads! Look at this!'

Lord Boothby recoiled in horror from the thing, hopping up onto Bad Bob's head to escape the beard's uncanny profusion. It was now well below his knees and in a few more seconds was piling up on the deck around his foot and wooden leg. Yards and yards of it – a great black, tangled mass, thick and coarse and wiry; a dense *bramble thicket* of a beard, creeping, crawling, twisting and twining, spreading out across the deck like a malevolent weed . . .

Robinson had not been lying when he'd expounded the properties of that potion (well, *mostly* not). At the bottom of the page on which the spell had been written, Sycorax had scrawled:

'Beware! Ye who *drink* the potion will suffer the *Abominable Beard!*'

And abominable that beard was.

Even diabolical . . .

It had reached the prostrate pirates now and had begun to curl and coil about their limbs.

'Somethin's got me!' screamed Sticky Tom. 'Somethin' 'orrible!'

And the others began to scream too as the beard swarmed about them, faster than an incoming tide.

Bad Bob was almost completely engulfed now. The beard spiralled around his body, encasing him in a hairy cocoon. Only the top of his head, where Lord Boothby flapped and hopped hysterically, and the upper portion of his face were visible atop a mountainous profusion of hair.

The look in his beady eye had changed. Gone was the fierce joy, the rapture and ecstasy of a dream fulfilled. Now, wild panic was there. Triumph had turned to disaster, delight to despair, dream to nightmare.

The beard was a monster.

He reached down among the hairy tendrils and, picking up his cutlass, began to hack at it, chopping great swathes of beard, as a harvester scythes a field of wheat.

But still, the beard continued to grow . . .

Chapter Sixty-One
A Ship In A Bottle

Jack watched, amazed, as the great ship shrank before his eyes. And because rather more than 'just a drop' of the potion had been used, it shrank dramatically and was but a few inches long when finally the shrinking stopped.

For a long minute he stared, open mouthed.

'How did you know?' he said, at last.

'Know what?' replied Robinson, equally impressed by the results of his magic spell.

'Know that Bad Bob *wanted* a beard.'

'Ah, I didn't. Not for sure. I had a hunch.'

'A jolly lucky hunch!'

'Indeed!'

Jack turned and looked up at Robinson, 'I doubted you, Robinson, just for a moment. I'm sorry. I thought you'd gone mad!'

'Well, it was a *bit* mad! But worth a try.'

A slight breeze suddenly began to ruffle the surface of the ocean, rocking the tiny ship wildly from side to side, and the seagull, which had been circling the shrinking ship with increasing curiosity, settled on the water beside it, just a few yards from the rowing boat. It opened its beak and reached down towards the tiny galleon.

'Oi! Get off!' cried Jack, grabbing an oar and waving it towards the bird. The seagull flew off with a cry of vexation. Jack dipped the oar into the water and gently guided the little ship towards the rowing boat. A bottle was floating in the water beside them – *The Lucky Bottle*, no doubt. Laying down the oar, Jack picked up the tiny ship with one hand and the empty bottle with the other.

'Whatever are you doing, Jack?' asked Robinson.

Jack made no reply. There had suddenly come upon him the same feeling he'd felt when seeing the tiny Hercules scrabbling around in the sand at Robinson's feet. He felt pity. Bad Bob and his pirates certainly didn't deserve his compassion – they would have killed him and Robinson without a second thought. But seeing the little ship at the mercy of the waves and the seagull and knowing that those pirates didn't stand a chance out there in the middle of the ocean, he suddenly felt sorry for them.

He pushed the tiny ship into the bottle, snapping the masts somewhat in the process. A cork bobbed in the water beside the rowing boat; it must have been the cork from the bottle of potion. Jack picked it up and pushed it into the top of the bottle. Then holding the bottle up before his eyes, he looked at the tiny ship within.

The sun had just dipped below the horizon, but Jack could just make out the pirates. He'd expected to see them staring up at his enormous face in terror, but they were not.

They were *fighting* – fighting among themselves! Or, at least, they appeared to be. He saw frenetic movement and the flash of cutlasses. And then he noticed an odd fuzziness about them. An odd fuzziness about the whole of the ship. He looked closer. It was all coming from one pirate: Bad Bob. More specifically, from his chin . . .

'It's a *beard*!' Jack cried. 'Bad Bob is growing an enormous beard, Robinson!'

'Why of course he is. You didn't think I was fibbing, did you?'

'But . . . but they're all *fighting* it! As if the beard is *attacking* them!'

'Indeed: it's the Abominable Beard!'

Jack looked confused.

'An unfortunate consequence of *drinking* the potion,' explained Robinson.

'But what will happen?'

'Oh, I daresay it will stop growing eventually. And with any luck Bad Bob will be left with a manageable amount still attached to his chin, which might cheer him up. On the other hand, I suspect he may well shave it all off and stick to having a chin as smooth as a baby's bottom . . .'

The light faded to darkness, and soon Jack could see no more. He put the bottle back in the water and said, 'Good luck! I hope *The Lucky Bottle* will be luckier for you fellows than it was for me. Though I suppose it *was* lucky for me in the end.'

He watched as the bottle drifted away into the night.

Chapter Sixty-Two
Home

'We'll still need a good dose of luck, Jack!' said Robinson, taking up the oars. 'Adrift in the middle of the ocean without water or provisions – we're by no means at the *end* of this adventure.'

But Jack only smiled. He was *feeling* lucky.

'Which direction, do you think?' asked Robinson.

Jack looked towards the afterglow of the sunset and then towards the darkness of the oncoming night.

'I think we should row into the dark,' he said. 'That way we'll meet the dawn quicker.' So they rowed to the east.

And they *were* lucky.

After rowing through the night, Robinson saw the sails of a ship, catching the first rays of the rising sun away on the southwestern horizon. He took off his shirt, tied it to an oar, and standing up, waved it like a flag above his head, calling:

'HAAALLLOOO THEEERE!'

His voice boomed out across the early-morning ocean.

Within twenty minutes the ship was alongside them and in five more they were standing on its deck, shaking hands with the captain, and drinking from a flask of cool, fresh water. They gave the captain a rather adapted version of their adventures; if they'd told him the whole truth, he most likely would not have believed a word of it. The ship was called *The Star of Cornwall* and was bound for Falmouth . . .

A few weeks later, Jack and Robinson found themselves standing on the quay at that port, listening to the rattle and creak of the wind blowing through the rigging of a hundred masts; and smelling the seaweedy, fishy smell of ports the world over.

Robinson was babbling away excitedly, pointing at this and that. Jack remained silent. The sights and smells had suddenly unlocked that part of him that he had tried to suppress for more than two long years. He was nearly overcome with emotion and found it impossible to speak.

He was almost home.

Presently Robinson looked down and seemed to understand Jack's mood. He stopped talking and, turning away, looked out to sea, half humming an old tune.

Then he said, 'I suppose it's time to say goodbye.'

Still lost in his memories, Jack remained silent, vaguely nodding without looking up.

'You'll be wanting to get off home, no doubt?' Robinson continued. 'I'm sure you know the way from here.' He put a hand on Jack's shoulder and said, 'Goodbye, Jack!'

Jack turned to him.

'What?'

'I'll be off,' said Robinson, with a shrug and a smile. 'I'm sure you're eager to get home. You must write, though, now you've learned the trick! Nice long letters with lots of news, please. And don't send them by bottle, for goodness' sake! I'll let you know my address as soon as I have one . . .'

'But . . . where are you *going?*'

'Oh, I don't know yet. I may sign up for a voyage on one of these ships, I may . . .'

'Don't be *silly*, Robinson!' cried Jack. 'You're coming home with me! You *must* come home with me!'

'But I couldn't do that, Jack. Your family won't want a big fellow like me around the place – they won't have room and–'

'Of course they will! They'll make room! I'll sleep in the barn, and you can have my room! Anyway – you *are* my family now. And my family is yours!'

'Really?' said Robinson, who looked as though he might shed a tear, so touched was he. 'Are you sure it would be all right?'

'Of course I am, Robinson! My home is your home!'

He flung his arms around Robinson's waist and Robinson, hugging Jack in return, *did* shed a tear.

Then Jack said, 'Come on!' and marched off.

They climbed a steep cobbled lane out of the town and inland towards the little valley where Jack had been born. All day, they tramped, along dusty roads overhung by trees and heavy with the scent of cow parsley, until the world opened out about them, and they were on the high moors. And as the sun dipped towards the horizon, they climbed the last hill and looked down upon fields where the grass was the greenest green ever, and amongst them, half concealed by encircling trees, they saw a grey stone farmhouse with a green front door.

Before the house, standing at the garden gate, they saw a woman. She clutched a shawl around her shoulders and looked out across the moor. When she saw the two figures coming over the hill above, her hand went to her mouth

and then she must have called out, for presently a man and
a young girl emerged from the green door, along with a cat
and a dog. The dog began to bark.

Jack began to run . . .

Epilogue

About six months after Jack and Robinson arrived at Falmouth, Old Ma Rollock was taking her early morning walk along the shore when something caught her eye. The glint of a glass bottle, just beyond the breaking waves.

'Page one hundred and sixty-one!' she cried and, hitching up her skirts, she splashed out into the surf to retrieve the missing instalment.

But it wasn't page 161.

Inside the bottle was something rather more curious. A tiny ship.

She wondered why anyone would put a little ship in a bottle. Little ships didn't really *fit* inside bottles. Indeed, whoever had put this one in, had broken all the masts. And yet, she had to admit, it was quite a novel idea, and straight away, she began to wonder how one might put a little ship into a bottle *without* breaking the masts . . .

Her hobby ever since she'd retired from innkeeping had been making model ships. There were hundreds of them, scattered about all over the cottage. There were also more than a hundred empty rum bottles . . .

By the end of that day, Old Ma Rollock had made the first prototype ship-in-a-bottle – with masts intact! Within a week, she was doing a brisk trade selling ships-in-bottles to all her neighbours. They became quite the thing to have sitting on one's mantelpiece in that corner of Cornwall . . . and very soon, in the wider world beyond.

And that is the story of how the whole ship-in-a-bottle thing got started, and though, in truth, it wasn't Old Ma Rollock who first thought of doing it, it was she who worked out how to get the ships into the bottles without breaking their masts.

How she did it, I've no idea!

The first bottle – the one she'd picked up from the sea – she placed, on its side, on the mantelpiece in her parlour. After a few days, she noticed a little pile of what looked like sawdust, just below the mouth of the bottle, and a thread hanging down from a tiny hole in the cork. She could almost swear there were tiny sawdust *footprints* tracing lines across the mantelpiece . . .

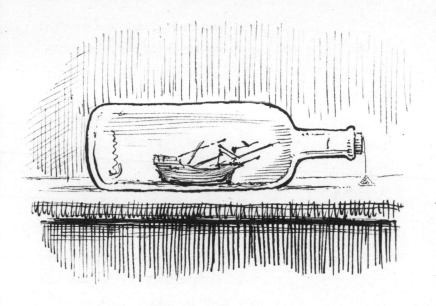

And then . . .

But that's a whole new story, and I'm afraid this book has
run out of pages!

Acknowledgements

Many thanks to my daughter, Eliza, who read the first completed draft of this story and gave it the thumbs up. To Mary, my wife, for many inspired suggestions, and to all at DFB, especially Alison Gadsby for putting the whole thing together, and my editors, Rosie and David Fickling, who helped enormously to refine and improve my long and rambling text.

Extract from

The MAGIC PLACE

Chris Wormell

Chapter One

Pepper

In the middle of a Great Black City of smoke and soot and grime there once lived a girl called Clementine.

Here is a picture of the Great Black City and down there under that bridge, at the far end of that dark narrow street, is the house where Clementine lives. Do you see it?

Clementine was an orphan and she lived in that tall narrow house with her Aunt and Uncle Grimble and a large white cat called

Gilbert. He was a rather special cat – in fact, he was an *extraordinary* cat, as we shall discover – and if you look again at the first picture you might spot him down under the bridge, as he walks along the road to that house down at the end. Let's follow him.

Outside the house he has stopped, and he peers into a dirty little window at the bottom of the wall, just above the pavement. What does he see?

He sees Clementine, sitting on the edge of her bed (for the dark and dingy cellar beyond that window is actually her bedroom). She has scruffy short

hair and wears a raggedy dress and shoes that are pretty much worn out.

And now she jumps up! She can hear the heavy clump of her aunt's footsteps descending the cellar stairs, and then the jingle of a large bunch of keys, as if a gaoler were lifting them from a belt. A key is slotted into the lock. The door handle begins to turn . . .

Clementine bites her lip. She lives in mortal fear of her terrible aunt . . .

Aunt Vermilia always wore black. And because of her poor eyesight she wore spectacles with such thick lenses her eyes looked enormous and appeared to jump out of her head. Clementine thought she looked like a large, fat beetle. Her Uncle Rufus had a very large mouth and lots of teeth, and Clementine thought *he* looked rather like a crocodile.

Would you like an aunt and uncle like these two?

No, neither would I.

And though looks can sometimes be deceptive, in this case they're not. These two were fiends. They were about as wicked and cruel as you could get. Uncle Rufus would sometimes beat Clementine with his heavy walking stick, while Aunt Vermilia often caught her by the ears and shook her head so violently it was a wonder her ears didn't come off! They were certainly stretched. At least, they *looked* stretched. Anyway, stretched or not, it was a horrible thing to do. Grabbing someone by the ear was about the meanest, cruellest thing Aunt Vermilia could think of doing to anyone – which just shows you what sort of person she was! And Clementine certainly didn't deserve it; she was not a naughty child. Not really. No more naughty than any child *ought* to be.

Though she did once 'accidentally' sprinkle a little pepper on their porridge.

5

Quite a lot of pepper actually.

But my goodness, they deserved it!

She was punished, of course. But then Clementine was *always* punished – whether she did anything bad or not. The slightest mistake would provoke an alarming outburst. Like accidentally dropping a single pea. And since it was she who did all the chores around the house – the cooking, the cleaning and all the washing up – she was bound to make the odd mistake.

She was even punished for things that were not her fault. If anything went missing in that house – or was broken or cracked or spilt or torn or spoilt – it was *always* blamed on Clementine (though it was very rarely her fault) and she was *always* punished.

Is it any wonder that she bit her lip in trepidation at the sound of her aunt's footsteps descending the cellar stairs?

And is it any wonder that she was sometimes driven to play little tricks on her wicked aunt and uncle? If she was going to be punished *anyway*, she thought, she may as well do something worth being punished for! And jolly good luck to her, I say.

I wonder why Clementine's Aunt and Uncle were so nasty? Perhaps they had had a horrible time when they were young?

'Little monster!' her Aunt Vermilia would scream. Or, 'Ogre!' Or, 'Vile little beast!'

7

And her Uncle Rufus would growl, 'Devil!', 'Demon!' and 'Rogue!'

All words that suited *them* far more than they suited Clementine. They hardly ever called her by her name. And when they did, they never called her Clementine. Do you know what they called her? They called her Oiya, which wasn't really a name at all, but came from them shouting, 'Oi, you!' whenever they wanted her. I suspect they didn't even know her real name *was* Clementine, which was odd.

But then neither did Clementine, which was odder.

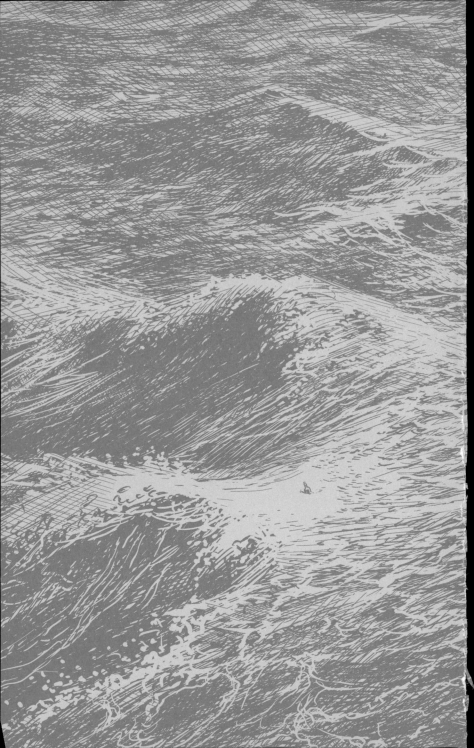